TRULY WANTED

Visit us at www.boldstrokesbooks.com

TRULY WANTED

by

J.J. Hale

2022

ISBN 13: 978-1-63679-333-7

THIS TRADE PAPERBACK ORIGINAL IS PUBLISHED BY
BOLD STROKES BOOKS, INC.
P.O. BOX 249
VALLEY FALLS, NY 12185

FIRST EDITION: OCTOBER 2022

CREDITS
EDITORS: JENNY HARMON AND CINDY CRESAP
PRODUCTION DESIGN: SUSAN RAMUNDO
COVER DESIGN BY TAMMY SEIDICK

Acknowledgments

Being both an ADHDer and Irish means making a long story short has never been my strong suit, so bear with me…

To Claire at Happy Tree Coaching, you were integral to me reaching my first dream of finishing this novel to begin with.

To everyone from the Bold Strokes Books team. Finishing a novel was my dream come true, getting to see it be published by my dream publisher was beyond anything I expected. A special thanks to my editor Jenny who made me feel at ease from our first phone call and understood my story, and me, right from the start. And even more unexpectedly, made the editing process genuinely enjoyable.

To my wife for supplying me with endless cups of tea, chocolate biscuits, and making sure I remember to eat and shower. Occasionally. Throughout my endless rotation of hobbies, writing is the one that's always stuck around and I'm thankful you help me find time to explore it.

To my little sidekicks who remind me every day that I can do anything…especially when they want me to do something for them. You better never read this.

To my sister, for being the Lexi to my Sam (except you're older, let's be clear on that). Just like them, we didn't choose to be sisters, but we did choose to be friends. Plus, you made very cute kids that I get to spoil.

To my (not so little) brother, who I'm thankful has the exact same terrible sense of humour as I do. You turned out pretty awesome, which was a pleasant surprise.

To my best friend who will always be my person. I'm thankful to you for many things but most importantly for introducing me, and in turn Sam, to Wynonna Earp.

To the awesome people I met on Twitter when I first dipped my toes into the writerly community. I've made so many friends who uplift me and each other daily, and who more importantly entertain me with memes or shout at me to write.

To Tigger, thank you for being a constant support in an ever-changing world. Your honest (and bratty) feedback and belief in me has meant more than you know. Plus, who else would listen to my daily ramblings from an ocean away and not change their number?

A special thanks to those who read the first very raw, messy version of this book—Meka, Charlie, Lily, Erica, Empi—your feedback and encouragement helped me develop this story into everything I hoped it could be.

Finally, a heartfelt thank you to the people who talk openly about ADHD and work so hard to build awareness. I wouldn't understand, or more importantly accept myself the way I do now if other people hadn't shared their stories so honestly. I hope Sam's story helps someone else feel a little more understood and a little less alone, just like I do.

Dedication

To my fellow Earpers, the original reason I joined Twitter before discovering the writing community was a thing. You are a wonderful example of the powers of community and positive representation. I am all in.

CHAPTER ONE

Then I tried cutting into the chicken with the ridiculously small knife, and next thing I know—"

Sam McKenna held her stomach, tears collecting at the corner of her eyes as her best friend mimicked the chicken breast flying across the restaurant floor. Sam's laughter carried on the light breeze.

It had been a couple of hours since Brooke had gotten back from her date. They spent the time rocking back and forth on the porch swing of Brooke's grey brick house, tea in hand and screen door open. Sam dropped her head back as her laughter subsided, staring at the starlit sky. That type of uncoordinated awkwardness was usually Sam's area of expertise, so it was nice to experience the embarrassment second-hand for once. The air turned cooler against her skin, after a rare, warm summer's day. They didn't get many of those in Ireland.

It was a good night. Being with her best friend was Sam's happy place, so despite the chill, she would have been content to sit for hours with Brooke and the beautiful night sky. Brooke suggested a movie with a visible shiver. Sitting on the porch or moving into the living room didn't matter to Sam, as long as she was with Brooke. She flopped on the couch as Brooke threw on an easy romance film. As per usual, most of the time was spent hashing out their own currently disastrous love lives, neglecting the on-screen plot.

The movie reached the confession part of the story, where both characters admitted their feelings and it closed in on happily ever after, and Sam heard Brooke sigh, her eyes suddenly glued to the screen.

"I'm never going to have that again."

Sam barely heard the whispered comment. She turned her head, frowning at the look of sadness clouding Brooke's face. "Don't be silly, B. One failed, clumsy date doesn't mean it won't happen."

Brooke shook her head. "No. I had my one true love with Jacob. That picture-perfect, oh-wow-I-love-you moment. The wedding that would've been perfect if my dad was still alive to walk me down the aisle. But even that was like a movie scene, with Jacob's dad stepping in, already more than a father-in-law to me. His family welcomed me from the moment I first met them and look at them now. It's been three years since his death and I'm still closer to his family than my own. Even if I did meet someone else, where do they fit into that?"

Sam reached out instinctively to hold Brooke's hand as she continued talking.

"I got my happily not so ever after. Then seven years, one kid, and one car accident later, he up and died. So now I'll spend the next forty years or whatever alone. At least I got my chance. Some people never do, I guess."

Sam noticed the tears that welled in Brooke's eyes. She pulled Brooke in and hugged her tight. "That's possibly one of the most ridiculous things you've ever said. Which is impressive since you say ridiculous things often."

Brooke's mouth opened wide as she pulled back and slapped Sam's arm lightly. "Way to kick a girl when she's down, Sammy."

Sam shook her head with a sigh. "Well, seriously. You think you're going to be alone? What am I, decoration? You think you're getting rid of me that easily? I have abandonment issues; we both know I'm not letting you out of my sight. Metaphorically, not stalker-ishly."

Brooke rolled her eyes. "That's different. You're my best friend. It's not the same."

"I'm your person. I'm always gonna be here. You'll wish you were alone when you get sick of me."

Brooke's smile was sad when she said, "You'll find someone. Look at you. Blond hair, gorgeous brown eyes, and a smile that sends every girl you aim it at swooning. Soon enough, you'll find your happily ever after, and then—"

"And then what?" Sam pressed. Frustration bubbled at the notion of Brooke thinking anything, or anyone would make her less important to Sam. "And then I leave you behind? Maybe that's now a contender for the most ridiculous thing you've said."

"Don't get mad at me, you know exactly what I mean. We're not together. We're not in love. We're not going to fall into bed together at the end of the night and wake up wrapped up in each other in the morning."

Her frustration was reflected back on Brooke's face. It didn't stop her stubborn reply though. "Actually, we've done that many times." Brooke threw her hands in the air. "Not with sex. We're not going to get married and live the rest of our lives together like them."

Sam turned to where Brooke pointed at the screen as the happy couple gazed gooey-eyed at each other after a long kiss. Her heart started to beat a little faster as the scene played out, similar to one that had run through her head many times before…starring her and the woman she sat beside.

She pulled her eyes from the television and back to Brooke, her mind still fixated on the fairy-tale ending she'd just witnessed on screen. Her mouth went dry, and she blurted out her next sentence before she even had time to fully form it in her brain.

"We could. I mean…maybe we should make a deal. If we're both single in, say, ten years, we can get married and live happily ever after together."

Her shrug was intended to lighten her words and she threw in a trademark grin as if it were the most logical idea in the world. Sometimes her impulsivity was a gift that allowed her to experience things or take chances before the anxious side of her brain could talk her out of them. But more often than not it just left her as surprised by what came out of her mouth as anyone else.

Brooke's glare didn't help Sam's heart rate return to its regular rhythm. "You're being ridiculous. This isn't the plot of a romance novel sitting on that shelf." She gestured vaguely at the bookshelf in the corner of the room. "Granted, it's totally one I would read. But stop joking around. I'm having an actual crisis here, I'm being serious."

"So am I," Sam countered. "We prefer being with each other more than anyone else in the world. I won't let you grow into an old spinster. I'd totally marry the shit out of you."

Brooke's look of frustration melted, and a grin tugged at her lips. "You're ridiculous," Brooke repeated, but her smile was growing as she shook her head.

The smile faltered as Brooke gulped, seemingly lost in her thoughts. "What's going on in that head of yours?" Sam asked.

Brooke's gaze darted around the room as she bit her lip before she suddenly blurted, "We don't even know if we are, you know, compatible."

Sam frowned. "Of course we are. We spend time together constantly. We love the same movies and books and talking about—"

Sam noticed Brooke's raised eyebrow and realized that's not what she meant. Heat crept up Sam's face as it dawned on her.

"Oh. Compatible. As in, like—"

Brooke nodded, taking over the conversation. "Sex. It's pretty important to me. To any marriage I intend to be in. I get it's not a big deal to everyone, but I like sex, despite the current lack of it in my life. Which you'd think would be less of an issue when my attraction ranges to all genders."

Sam nodded, but her throat was suddenly extremely dry. Unlike other, more southern parts of her body. Even Brooke's sexuality joke didn't lighten the pounding of her heart. This line of conversation was…doing things to her. To be fair, it had been far too long since she'd last been with anyone, so it didn't take much these days. Before the past few years, Sam had plenty of experience falling into bed with women. But it had been a long time since any of those women knew anything about her past the surface level. Not one of them had known her like Brooke.

Sam let her eyes travel down Brooke's body beside her on the couch. She rarely allowed herself the chance to focus on Brooke in this way. Of course, she knew Brooke was hot; she didn't need to pay much attention to notice that. Sam thought back to college when she first laid eyes on Brooke and fell into instant crush mode. Her cool ivory skin, wavy brown hair, and deep blue irises were a combination that made Sam's mouth water the first time she took them in. Combined with full lips and a killer body, Brooke was a knockout.

Sam gulped. The crush had never fully left. She had just gotten very good at ignoring those feelings after she was introduced to Brooke's boyfriend. Being Brooke's best friend was much more important than anything else. But for just a moment, she allowed herself to drink in the body she knew so well and yet, not at all.

Sam imagined her lips pressed against the soft curve of Brooke's neck. Her eyes travelled along Brooke's jawline as she considered how it would feel to press her lips against each inch of skin that currently captured her attention. She watched as Brooke's teeth grazed against her bottom lip and Sam lifted her gaze to Brooke's, which was focused on her. Eyes that were usually an open book to Sam were currently hard to read.

Heat flooded Sam's cheeks even more as she doubted her own lusty thoughts were as well hidden on her face. Her heart beat faster as Brooke cocked her head to the side, the unforgiving silence enveloping them. *What the hell was happening?* Sam's thoughts went into overdrive and she knew she needed to get out of there before her impulses landed her in a situation that could irreversibly change life as she knew it.

This wouldn't be some random hook-up. Sam made sure she was always the one to leave so her fear of rejection never got a chance to kick in. But this wasn't some woman she could easily forget, this was Brooke, the one person she never wanted to walk out on.

Sam managed a few well-timed yawns and made her excuses to go to bed early. Brooke didn't protest, clearly as flustered as Sam was. She had her own room at Brooke's and often stayed over. She practically moved in for the first year following the car accident that killed Jacob. After she crawled under the covers, she turned on her side and curled into the blanket. She glanced at the photo frame Brooke had gifted her on her birthday earlier in the year. It was a photo of them taken by a stranger at the zoo, Brooke's arm around her waist, the biggest smile lit up her face.

Sam closed her eyes and retreated under the covers with nothing but thoughts of Brooke's smile aimed at someone else. The same thoughts that had been haunting her for months now, watching Brooke go on date after date, her heart panging more each time. The feelings she had shut down for so long had come bubbling to the surface recently and Sam needed to get a handle on it.

The lust that engulfed her moments ago quickly fled, making room for the dull ache she knew too well. One she couldn't put a name to for so many years of her life, until she finally decided to stop fighting her neurodivergent brain on a daily basis and learn more about how it worked. When she first heard the term rejection sensitive dysphoria while researching about her ADHD, a lot of puzzle pieces clicked into place.

That overwhelming sadness that hit when she felt rejected. The irrational anger. The embarrassment that made everyday interactions difficult to navigate. She ticked every box. By now, she knew when it started, she had to ride it out. It usually didn't last long, but the intensity never wavered. Closing her eyes, she ran through the mantras she'd learned. The ways to remind herself she wasn't being rejected, she wasn't being abandoned, she was safe.

It was a big part of her fear of relationships. How did you get somebody to understand something they had never experienced, something she didn't understand herself for so long? Brooke got it though. Somehow, Brooke always understood what she needed. That's why the thoughts she was having earlier needed to go back into the box they'd quietly stayed in for a decade.

Sam made a pact with herself that night. She would move on. She would make an effort to find someone, the way Brooke was trying to. The past few years had lulled her into a comfortable routine, her focus had been solely on work and being here, in this house, with the only family she had ever known. Brooke was her best friend and had been through a lot; she needed Sam. But now it was time for Sam to put herself first and try to move on from this silly crush.

Even if she knew deep down that it was so much more than that.

❖

Brooke Fields sat on her grey leather couch long after Sam's made-up excuse to go to bed. She was kicking herself for the way the night had ended. *Why had she said that?* Being compatible in that way with Sam was so far beyond any realm of thought she'd ever had before it had been a shock to hear the words leave her lips. She sipped the new cup of tea she had made an hour ago and wrinkled her nose as she swallowed the far too cold liquid. *Was it really that ridiculous a thought?*

Sam's suggestion of a marriage pact had been totally out of left field. Even though Sam tried to play if off as a joke, the words had sparked something in Brooke. A curiosity she'd never before considered. It was like somebody flipped a switch and suddenly, she saw Sam in a totally new light.

It seemed like just yesterday she was trying to get Sam to entertain a friendship with her. Brooke smiled to herself as she remembered how captivated she had been by the stubborn, independent girl who was worlds apart from any of the peers she'd grown up with. Most of the people she'd grown up around cared about status, money, and power. But Sam? Sam had none of that and didn't care about attaining it either. Brooke closed her eyes and allowed herself a trip down memory lane to distract herself from the confusion of the night.

It was halfway through her first year of college, and Brooke was struggling to understand half of what the lecturer was saying in this Computer Programming class. Her forte was much more the business side of the Business Information Systems course. When the lecturer said they'd be doing a group assignment, she sighed in relief. Most people seemed to hate them, but there was no chance she'd get this assignment done alone when it involved skills she just never seemed to be able to master. She excelled at the organization side of these projects, though.

Liam, the guy who sat next to her every class as she pretended not to notice him ogling her, turned and scooched his chair closer. Apparently, they were going to be partners. Her eyes roamed desperately around the room, hoping for some barrier between them, when they landed on a girl who looked like a deer caught in headlights.

Brooke beckoned her over, saying a silent prayer that she would respond, and sighed in relief when after a moment the girl made her way toward them. Brooke had been in this class for at least half a year and she couldn't remember seeing this girl before. Her blond hair was pulled back in a messy ponytail, her jeans were ripped, and not the on-purpose kind, and her T-shirt looked slept in. But what stood out to Brooke most were the honey brown eyes that seemed glued to hers.

"Hey, I'm Brooke. This is Liam. You looked like you could use a group, and we could use a third."

The girl introduced herself as Sam and Brooke quickly realized she had made a great choice. Sam was brilliant. Smart, funny, and a million times better than Brooke at the coding side of this project. Sam was also perceptive. It didn't take her long to pick up on Liam's lack of interest in the actual project, and Brooke's discomfort. Especially when his persistence didn't waver, despite Brooke's frequent mentions of her boyfriend.

Sam made sure to always insert herself between them and it didn't take long for Liam to stop showing up to their group sessions altogether. Brooke was grateful. She was surprised to find, while working with Sam and without the extra distraction, that she was starting to understand far more than she ever had before. Midway through the project she was able to follow along as Sam turned the designs they agreed upon into an actual website. Brooke looked forward to their time together and she could tell Sam did too.

Before college, Brooke was used to making friends and being popular based on what she had to offer. The school she attended was prestigious and expensive, and Brooke always felt like she had to prove her worth there. Sam didn't seem to care about what Brooke could offer. She would light up anytime Brooke needed help with something, taking time to explain in ways that made sense to Brooke.

When Brooke made a comment about feeling like she'd never get it, Sam reminded her how much she'd already understood over their few weeks as friends. And that's what they had become, friends. That was solidified even more when Sam confided in Brooke about having ADHD. Sam seemed fearful telling her, which made Brooke wonder how often the revelation was met with negativity. If anything, Brooke was just happy she could pay Sam back for all the help Sam had given her already.

A lot of the things Sam spoke about struggling with, time keeping, forgetfulness, motivation, were things Brooke excelled at. They got into a great rhythm. Brooke managed the project, helped Sam keep track of her notes and their deadlines, and Sam continued to help Brooke actually learn the subject. They worked so well together they got the project done early. Brooke was relieved and looked forward to hanging out with Sam without having to focus on work.

That was, until Sam disappeared from her life as quickly as she had entered it.

There never seemed to be a good time to meet up. Sam's replies had gone from detailed and friendly to barely a sentence. She always got to class just late enough to avoid sitting near Brooke. It didn't make any sense. Brooke worried she had done something, but she couldn't think what it could be. Her gut was telling her this was more about Sam than her, and her gut was rarely wrong.

Brooke was nothing if not stubborn. She worried about intruding on Sam's life, but from the time they'd spent together, she also knew Sam didn't have anyone else in it. If Sam didn't want a friend, Brooke would respect that, but she had to at least give it one last shot. For her own peace of mind. Sam had left a mark and Brooke couldn't walk away from that without knowing she gave it her all. So, she grabbed beer and pizza from a local place and headed to Sam's dorm room.

Brooke stood there, about to turn and walk away as nerves got the better of her until Sam opened the door. Sam's brow furrowed in confusion as she took in the sight and Brooke launched into a rambling version of her rehearsed speech.

"I realize I'm bordering on stalker level now, but here goes. I enjoy spending time with you, Sam. I don't know exactly why you withdrew, but I have a feeling it's less to do with me and more to do with you. So, if I'm wrong, here's a pizza that you can enjoy by yourself, and I can disappear. But if I'm not, we can share a pizza and talk or not talk, whichever you prefer."

Sam stood at the door; mouth agape, and Brooke chastised herself. It was too much. She had gone too far. Then, right as she was about to apologize and leave, Sam moved aside for Brooke to walk in.

Sam had let Brooke in that night, both to her room and her life. It took time for Sam to take down her walls and trust Brooke, but she did. She trusted Brooke with the details of her life, so many of which explained exactly why she had withdrawn. Sam wasn't used to people trying for her. She wasn't used to people sticking around long enough to see the amazing person she was. Brooke vowed back then to make sure Sam knew she wasn't going anywhere and to make Sam feel as understood as she made Brooke feel.

Brooke was exhausted. The memories were welcome, but emotional. They reminded her why entertaining any ideas of jeopardizing her friendship with Sam was ridiculous. Sam often told the story as if Brooke came to her that night in college because she thought Sam needed somebody. When in reality, it was always Brooke that needed Sam more. And that had never changed. Now it was time for Brooke to push her silly daydreams aside and make sure she kept her vow instead of sending Sam fleeing.

CHAPTER TWO

The sun was still high in the sky as Sam left work. She raked her fingers through her hair and peered through the window of the store. The lights were definitely off, she reminded herself. She didn't have time to recheck today. She gripped the handles of her backpack as she walked down a side street toward the bus stop. She never drove to work; parking was a nightmare, and she liked the free time to read or think on the bus journey.

The bus pulled up mere minutes after Sam arrived at the stop. She slouched in her usual seat, and her thoughts wandered to Brooke, who had taken up most of her brain space the past week after their conversation. Apparently, the mere thought of anything more with Brooke last week had popped Pandora's box right open, and now Sam's hormones were getting out of control. All week long, thoughts of exactly how compatible she and Brooke could be kept her mind and body awake far too late. Even on the bus, her body had an immediate visceral response as Brooke's face flashed before her eyes. Followed by her smile, her curves, her perfect—

Shit. That was her stop. Luckily, the next stop was only a few minutes out of her way. She got off the bus and walked back to her apartment, chastising herself for her way too vivid imagination. She didn't have time for delays after her last client meeting ran over and held her up.

She turned the key in the lock and threw her bag down as she stepped into her apartment. Living alone had a lot of benefits, namely that she didn't have to deal with people once she got home. After years of sharing rooms and sometimes even beds, having a place to call hers and hers alone was like heaven. Sure, being alone had its pitfalls, but she had been alone while surrounded by people for most of her life, and this was by far preferable.

Growing up in foster care meant she was used to fending for herself. She'd had some good foster parents along the way but more were indifferent, and occasionally downright awful. Appreciating the good ones was hard when she was so jaded by the negative experiences. Her ADHD meant foster families had to put forth more effort than most were willing to. When they got called in to school one too many times because Sam couldn't stop talking, interrupting the teacher, couldn't sit still or wait her turn, or when she eventually lashed out when the other kids picked on her for once again being the new kid, they usually came to the conclusion that it was much easier to schlep her off to a new family.

The constant change of carers got even trickier as she grew older. Some encouraged her medication, some did not, some overdid the meds to keep her quiet, some refused it altogether. It was hard enough to settle into a new place and to be in a stranger's house. To learn all about them and be aware that they knew all about you. But to do that while wondering if they blamed you and resented you for the way your brain works? It was impossible. Sam never knew whom to trust, which meant she learned to trust no one.

That was until Brooke came along. Sam's gaze landed on the photo frame displayed on a shelf to the right of her television. Her own blond hair was slightly longer in the photo than now, but Brooke looked exactly the same. Simultaneously, her heart and the sensitive flesh between her legs ached as thoughts of Brooke's body invaded her mind, and she knew her efforts to resist were futile. She had no choice but to take care of her current state before she left, or the night would be a total disaster before it even began.

She kicked off her shoes and undressed, leaving a trail of clothes behind her on the way to the bathroom. Another thing she loved about living alone. Nobody around to judge her messiness as if it were a moral failing. She turned the knob in the shower and made sure the temperature was right before she slipped under the cascading water. Her skin still tingled from her daydreams as she let her hand wander down between her legs. No time to romance herself today. Straight to the end goal.

Sam stroked her most sensitive spot as she allowed herself to imagine her back pressed to the shower glass, palms flat against the surface, with Brooke on her knees, tongue taking the position Sam's fingers currently occupied.

With that image in mind, it didn't take long before a familiar sensation travelled up her legs and curled in her abdomen, her release welcome but nowhere near enough. But it would have to do.

She continued with her shower and got dressed, anxiety making her antsy. She packed a bag with her essentials, clothes, chargers, and the new toy and movie she had picked up for tonight. Her step quickened as she grabbed her car keys and left.

As Sam turned her car into the driveway twenty minutes later, she spied them through the window, her mouth turning upward in an involuntary grin. Brooke's back was to her, and Sam took a moment to ogle her perfect ass before shaking her head and chastising herself. Time to snap out of it.

She got out of the car and headed to the door, walking right through as she always did. Footsteps thundered toward her immediately. Arms were wrapped around her waist before she had time to blink and a piercing shout announced, "Aunt Sammy is here. Mama, Aunt Sammy!"

Brooke appeared from around the corner and shook her head with a grin. "Yes, Finley, she sure is."

Their eyes locked, and Brooke rolled hers.

"My kid adores you almost as much as I do. Thanks so much again for tonight. I know it was short notice."

Sam's heart squeezed in her chest and she smiled. "I adore your kid, too. I think you're all right."

Brooke rolled her eyes once more, her usual response to Sam's attempts at humor.

"Are you okay with him if I go finish getting ready?"

Sam nodded, and Brooke went upstairs. To get ready. For her date. Just like she had almost monthly for the past year. Just like she had last week. Sam tried to shake off the sudden surge of wanting.

Finley tugged on Sam's leg and snapped her out of her thoughts.

She sighed, grabbed the excited three-year-old, and plopped him over her shoulder as his giggles soothed her aching heart.

❖

Brooke took her time getting ready as she listened to the two people who mattered most in the world to her playing downstairs. Sam had remained her best friend since that first year of college. She had been there through everything, the good times and bad. Especially the bad. Now here she was, giving up another Friday night to watch Finley, as Brooke went on yet another date and tried to force herself to move on from Jacob.

Her thoughts wandered back to last week and the conversation between them. For a minute she had considered…Her body tingled with the memory, but Brooke shut it down in her mind. She and Sam were just friends. Best friends.

It was for the best; she couldn't risk losing Sam. She turned her thoughts to her date. She worried about calling on Sam to babysit just a week after her last date. But everything had been so weird the next morning, Brooke wanted to show them both that she was putting herself out there. With other, far more appropriate, people.

It eased her conscience to know that Sam adored Finley, and Finley loved Sam almost as much as he did Brooke. More, she was sometimes convinced when she took in scenes like the one she witnessed when she walked into the room.

Sam was sprawled on the couch and Finley curled on her lap with a look of pure contentment on his face, as they watched yet another new movie and he clutched a new stuffed toy. She shook her head at Sam's spoiling of her son, but Brooke couldn't bring herself to reprimand her. Not tonight.

Brooke sighed and gazed longingly at the couch, the bowl of popcorn, the familiar faces. She could lose herself all too quickly in the comfort. Her heart tugged toward Sam, along with a lingering spark of the newfound attraction she was trying so hard to quash. As she checked her watch, she shook herself from her daze. Time to get a move on.

She cleared her throat and Sam glanced up. She didn't miss the widened eyes or the quick appraisal of her outfit. Upstairs while she looked in the mirror, Brooke's self-consciousness crept in. Was her outfit okay? Was it too casual, too dressy? She had spent so long trying to make herself feel comfortable with her body, but dating made it harder not to worry.

However, the look Sam sported as she took in her heels, black jeans, and blue wrap top gave Brooke's confidence the boost it needed. She allowed herself one moment to bask in the unspoken compliment and then shook it off. It didn't matter. Sam was way too precious to allow simple lust to get in the way.

"Fin, be a good boy and take care of Aunt Sam. Make sure she brushes her teeth and gets to bed on time."

Finley grinned up at her, the smile a mirror image of his father's. The comparison didn't hurt as much as it used to Brooke noticed, as she planted her lips on his forehead.

"Good luck. Try to make it back in one piece. Watch out for flying poultry!" Sam grinned.

Brooke once again rolled her eyes, but her smile widened, nonetheless. "I'll do my best. Try not to let the kid wrap you around his little finger."

They both laughed. It was much too late for that.

She grabbed her car keys off the hook and walked out the door, not turning back to survey the scene because if she did, there was a good chance she wouldn't make it to her date. It wouldn't be the first time she'd cancelled to bask in the comfort of Sam.

As Brooke pulled into the parking lot of the bar where she had arranged to meet her date for a drink before dinner, she took a breath. Putting herself out there was getting pretty exhausting. But the niggling fear in the back of her mind of ending up alone pushed her into action, and she climbed out of the car.

Her eyes locked onto the redhead who occupied a stool at the bar as she walked through the door. Luckily, this time, the photo had been a recent and accurate portrayal. As she approached, their eyes met, and something akin to butterflies fluttered in her stomach. Maybe this wouldn't be so bad.

"Dani?" Brooke enquired, despite knowing the answer.

The other woman's lips lifted in a smile that made her eyes look an even brighter shade of blue. Her pale white skin contrasted beautifully with the vibrance of her hair, a smattering of freckles dotted across her cheeks. Brooke briefly flashed to Sam and the freckles that adorned her face. The cheeky smirk on her lips that made the freckles around the dimple on her cheek stand out even more.

She caught herself just in time to hear the woman in front of her, the one she should be focused on, reply.

"Yes. Brooke, nice to finally meet you."

She needed to stay in the present and direct her attention on the attractive woman she was here to meet. Online dating was weird. You chatted with someone before ever meeting so you knew random, small talk information about them and occasionally even deeper, personal stories but not what they truly looked or sounded like in person.

Last week's date was an accountant named Ted who was about as interesting as he sounded. She shouldn't stereotype, but he really hit every box. Her chicken flying across the restaurant livened up the evening. She ended up home and chilling with Sam in no time, which, given what transpired after, had spurred her on to arrange meeting Dani this week when the opportunity arose.

She pulled her mind back before it wandered down the road of last week's conversation, as it had many times since at inappropriate moments.

Before Ted was Karla, who was beautiful, funny, and absolutely hated children. That was one she got away from before dessert. Dani, however, said all the right things, laughed in all the right places, and before Brooke knew it, her dessert plate was empty in front of her and she was reluctant to leave.

They lingered and chatted. Dani leaned in to listen intently as Brooke spoke, giving her full attention to the conversation. Even when the topic of Finley came up, as Brooke regaled her with a story of their latest trip to the beach with Sam, Dani asked questions about Fin and spoke about her nieces and nephews and how much she adored them. Although Brooke would never introduce a date to her son until she knew it was the right time, it was good to know from the start that it was a possibility. Brooke was a package deal, and she would never hide that.

They figured out they went to the same college, only a year apart. It wasn't a surprise since there was exactly one university in their city. Ireland wasn't a big place, so online dating was even dicier when chances were, you'd have some connection to the person. The last thing you wanted was to have an awful date and find out you'd have to see them again.

"Well, when I met my best friend in college, it was also during a disastrous group project. So, some good does come from them occasionally. But I agree they are a test of patience most of the time." Dani's hand landed on her arm as she laughed at Brooke's words and Brooke's skin tingled even when the contact was over. This was going far better than she could've expected.

"Let me guess. Sam?" Brooke nodded at Dani's reply and continued, explaining the story of the horny third member of their group who disappeared when he figured out Sam wasn't letting him any closer to Brooke. She barely remembered his name now, but his absence ended up being a gift in the end.

When the night came to an end, Dani walked Brooke to her car and briefly squeezed her hand and spoke softly. "I had a great time tonight."

The sky was dark apart from the glow of the streetlamps. The warmth in Brooke's chest had nothing to do with the air and everything to do with the woman standing in front of her. She had a good feeling about Dani, and her good feelings were rarely mistaken. She thought back again to meeting Sam in college and how she knew in an instant they were meant to be in each other's lives. Her intuition usually proved her right.

"Me too," Brooke replied, this time not having to lie. They both smiled, and she decided to just go for it. As the words left her lips, Dani spoke at the same time, cutting her off.

"I'd love to see you a—"

"We'd be great as friends."

Brooke frowned at Dani's words, the puzzle pieces not adding up in her head. She'd been sure they were on the same page all night. Warmth spread up her neck to her cheeks and she was grateful for the dark of the night that covered her embarrassment.

"Look Brooke, you're great. Really. I think we have so much in common. This online dating thing is a minefield and I've rarely met someone I've talked with at such ease all night. If it wasn't for the fact that you're clearly in love with your best friend, we could probably have something. But that's not a situation I want to get caught up in. So, friends?"

The air caught in Brooke's lungs and she scrambled to find the words she wanted to say.

"Wait, what? No. Sam is my best friend, but I'm not in love with her."

Dani's eyebrow raise said more than her words. Her eyes were soft, understanding, and held not a hint of annoyance or anger. This woman was definitely someone Brooke wanted to know more about.

"I probably know more about Sam than I do about you, Brooke. You've managed to bring her up in almost every conversation all night. Clearly, she's been running through your mind. Don't get me wrong, I loved our dinner and conversation, but when a woman on a first date doesn't shut up about another woman? That's a pretty clear sign that you're going to get your heart broken and I'm not here for heartbreak."

Brooke was stumped. Sam was a big part of her life. She hadn't meant to talk about her so much, and hadn't realized she was, but it was natural Sam would come up when they spent so much time together. Right? Dani squeezed her hand again and reiterated the part about being friends before she got in her car and drove off.

Brooke sat for what seemed like an hour, turning the night over in her head. It was ridiculous. She couldn't be in love with Sam. *Could she?* No. It was that silly conversation and the curiosity that surged because of it. That was all.

Dani was an amazing woman, how had she managed to blow this on the first night? She shook herself off and started the car. She would make sure the next date she went on, Sam's name never left her lips.

On the drive home, her thoughts turned to Sam, who would undoubtedly be waiting up to hear about another disastrous date. Her gut clenched unpleasantly but she shook it off. Sam would be happy for her that she'd had a good night. But how would she explain why they weren't going to see each other again? She couldn't tell her the truth. Maybe before the previous week, they would have laughed over the absurdity of it. But she didn't want Sam to worry that she was responsible for ruining Brooke's chances. Or worse, that Brooke might risk their friendship for…for what?

Sam had been saying all year how she wanted Brooke to find someone who would appreciate her as Jake did. Someone worthy of loving her. Someone who would treat Brooke and Finley the way they deserved to be treated. And most importantly, Sam would joke, someone who made Brooke feel like a horny, lovesick teenager again.

There was already someone who did all of those things. All except the last. Until now.

CHAPTER THREE

Sam flicked through channels while trying not to check the clock on her phone for the tenth time in fifteen minutes. She had no interest in the programs that played. Her anxiety increased exponentially with each time check. Brooke was always home by now.

Sam's fatalistic brain imagined various scenarios. She got kidnapped. Drugged. She was hurt and alone. Car crash, that was possible. Sam didn't allow herself to imagine the most likely outcome. That Brooke was just...enjoying herself.

She knew the absurdity of what had just gone through her head. Was she seriously considering her best friend hurt or kidnapped preferable to having a good date? Of course not. She wanted Brooke to have fun.

This was usually the part of the night that Sam anticipated most. Brooke would get back, they'd sit with tea and snacks, and Brooke would bitch about how awful her date was. Sam would make terrible jokes, Brooke would roll her eyes but laugh nonetheless, and everything would feel right. She had a feeling that wouldn't happen tonight.

Sam chastised herself. She needed to get a grip. Brooke and Finley were the best things in her life. They weren't just friends; they were her family. She couldn't mess that up for anything, not even a chance at more.

It hadn't always been this difficult. Her feelings had been easy to keep at bay when Jake was around. He meant almost as much to Sam as Brooke did, and they were perfect together. It was easy to play the part of the supportive best friend then.

Keys jingled in the door and Sam released a sigh of relief. As messed up as her intrusive thoughts could be, knowing Brooke was safe was of utmost importance. Brooke's heels clicked as she walked into the living room. How she managed to walk in those things Sam would never know, or care to find out. Converse were her best friend, and that's how it would remain.

The sheepish smile on Brooke's face and the soft "Hey" made Sam's heart ache. Usually, Brooke was flicking on the kettle and complaining about how her feet ached at this point. Tonight, she looked…smitten. Sam braced herself for what was to come. Might as well get it over with.

"Good night?"

Brooke walked over and plopped down next to her on the couch. "Yeah, it was actually."

She sounded hesitant and Sam frowned. "But…"

Sam knew it was awkward, but Brooke never had an issue telling her about dates in the past. They needed to be normal. Granted, generally, Brooke was talking about bad ones, but she should be gooey and gushing if her face was anything to go by.

"No but. It was good. She was…nice. "

Sam took a leaf out of Brooke's book and rolled her eyes. "Are you describing your date, or dinner, because honestly, you've had more enthusiastic conversations about food in the past. Was it good? Your face says yes."

Brooke seemed to have some sort of internal battle going on in her head before she shook herself and turned. "You're my best friend, you know that? I love spending this time with you."

Sam's frown deepened. She wasn't sure where this was going, but she had a feeling it was nowhere good. The familiar creeping ache tried to make its way into her chest before she shut it down.

"I know that, goof, now stop delaying telling me about this date. I wanna know all the gooey details."

That was the last thing Sam wanted to know, but anything was preferable to the intense look Brooke gave her. Did Brooke feel sorry for her? Because she had a good date and Sam had no one?

Sam's insides turned sour at the thought. Pity was the one thing she never wanted to be directed at her. Her life could've been a pity party for one if she had let it go down that path, but she vehemently refused. She had built an amazing life for herself from scratch, one she was proud of, and single or not, she was happy. She refused to let anyone feel sorry for her. Plus, this was Brooke. Through everything they'd shared, pity had never played a part. Sam needed to trust her the way the logical part of her knew Brooke deserved.

"Brooke, seriously, you don't have to worry about my feelings. I'm happy if you're happy. As long as you still play wingwoman for me on occasion, I'm good. Now spill."

Brooke frowned slightly and her eyes glazed over briefly. Then, her smile widened, and finally, she relayed the events of the night, in all their gloriously heart-wrenching detail. Sam was right on the money earlier. Brooke was smitten.

"We got on really well, but we both agreed the attraction wasn't there. I'm really glad I went though, I feel like she's going to be a great friend." Sam did a double take at Brooke's words. That sentence did not match the retelling of the date before it.

"I'm confused, because that face is not the face of someone who's lacking attraction." She pointed her finger at Brooke to emphasize her point. "And those are not eyes holding purely innocent, friendly thoughts."

She raised her eyebrow as a hint of pink made its way onto Brooke's cheeks and her eyes darted around. "I…like her. I do. It's just confusing."

"Oh yes, I can see why going on a nearly perfect first date with a seemingly gorgeous woman who loves kids and makes you have dirty thoughts is so confusing. Makes total sense."

Brooke threw a cushion at Sam and they laughed.

All the while, Sam knew that this was different. This person had affected Brooke in a way that Sam hadn't seen in, well, almost three years. Sam wanted more than anything to feel good for her. She wanted Brooke to be happy again, to have the glow she always had when Jake walked into a room. But her heart just wasn't in it this time. A door she had worked hard to keep firmly shut had flown open. Hearing her talk about her date only confirmed it.

Brooke seemed adamant about the *just friends* part. She said that Dani thought it was best and that Brooke agreed. She repeated that they had a great time but lacked chemistry for anything more than a good friendship. Which sounded like bullshit to Sam. She worried Brooke was trying to spare her feelings, maybe ease into things more casually. This woman seemed perfect for Brooke and there was no way Sam would let her own jealousy or ego ruin that. She was determined to make sure Brooke didn't self-sabotage.

Right after she had a chance to lick her own wounds.

❖

Brooke woke up the next morning to a three-year-old demanding breakfast and a text on her phone from Dani. She smiled, and the warmth in her stomach was a welcome feeling.

"Had a great time last night. Sorry if I overstepped with what I said. I really do think we should be friends. I have no idea how to make friends as an adult so, if I promise to keep my Sam-related opinions to myself, do you want to grab lunch during the week?"

After a tickle attack on Finley, she carried him down to the kitchen and set him up with some cereal. She took her phone out to reply, a lingering smile still on her face. Brooke was happy she had made a friend. Dani was right, the etiquette around friend making was always dicey as an adult. She certainly wouldn't waste the opportunity when it presented itself.

"Somebody is in a good mood."

Sam sauntered into the kitchen and smacked a kiss on Finley's cheek before she made herself the same overly sugary cereal. Brooke smiled. Not much had changed over the years, and certainly not Sam's sweet tooth.

"Yes, me, Sammy, I'm in a good mood!" Finley showed off the biggest toothy grin to prove his point.

"You're always in a good mood when you're with me, kiddo." She winked at him and Brooke watched the interaction fondly. She loved how close they were. She loved her family.

Her heart ached that Jacob wasn't here, that Finley didn't have his dad to share moments like this with. She worried about raising him alone, but she worried even more about feeling like she was replacing his father. She knew what kind of dad Jacob would've been if he had been given the chance. The kind Brooke had grown up with. After her parents divorced and her mom moved away, apart from infrequent visits, her dad raised her alone.

The day she found out her father had been diagnosed with stage four pancreatic cancer was one of the hardest of her life. It was a few short months later that he died. She'd been dating Jacob only a couple of months at the time, and he was her rock throughout it all. She cherished every moment she had gotten with her father. She hated that Finley didn't have those memories to look back on with Jacob.

Surveying the scene in front of her, she knew he had two people who loved and cherished him more than anything. Sam would give the world for Finley. Brooke was so grateful for that, but the niggling fear of forgetting about Jacob was there in the recesses of her mind. She glanced at her son again, and the eyes a carbon copy of his father's were so full of joy that Brooke couldn't help but smile. She couldn't forget Jacob with a living reminder in Finley. She wouldn't.

Sam caught her eye and cocked her head to the side. "What's going on in that head of yours, Fields?"

Brooke smiled as milk dribbled down Sam's chin. "I was thinking about my dad. He loved silly jokes almost as much as you do."

Sam pointed her spoon at Brooke as she replied, "My jokes are superb I'll have you know." She nudged Finley for backup as she continued, "Your son thinks they are the best."

Brooke rolled her eyes. "My son is three and finds poop hilarious."

Sam shrugged, "That's because it is."

Brooke shook her head and laughed, focusing her gaze back on her phone. What was she doing again? Oh right, yes, Dani. She typed out a quick reply about meeting for lunch during the week and suggested Tuesday. She put her phone in her pocket, grabbed her cup of tea from the counter, and joined Sam and Finley, still goofing off, at the table. Sometimes she was convinced she had two children to look after.

A little while later as Sam got ready to leave, she approached Brooke. "Next Friday. Wingwoman duties?"

Sam shifted on her feet and toyed with the keys in her hand, refusing to make eye contact with Brooke as she spoke. Brooke got a weird feeling in her gut. It had been a while since Sam had requested this.

"Of course. I'll ask Maddie to take Finley, I'm sure she'll love spoiling him without me around. Just let me know a time and place."

She put a smile on her face that she didn't feel and hugged Sam just a little tighter than necessary. She wasn't sure where the unpleasant sensation that washed over her came from. She was the one who had bugged Sam to put herself out there more. With the amount of time Sam put into her and Finley, Brooke often worried about being partly responsible for Sam's single status. She should be trying to find her own great love story, even if that meant less time with Brooke. Her jealousy at not having Sam all to herself was unfair, and she didn't like it.

After Sam left, she shut the door and leaned back against it, taking a moment. She'd had a date with a wonderful woman last night. A woman without complications, without risk. A woman who was wildly attractive, smart, and funny. Yet here she was, feeling things she shouldn't be feeling because Sam wanted to find someone too.

She was just used to Sam being around, being there for her and Finley. She was worried that would change if someone new came on the scene. She was being selfish. She wouldn't let herself entertain the fact that maybe, just maybe, Dani had a point.

Brooke would be sure to do her best to find someone worthy of Sam, who deserved the wonder Sam brought into everyone's life. The way she could make you feel like you were the most important person in the world. Her ability to remember the smallest details of your interests and put them to use in the most thoughtful of ways. How she found humor and light even in the darkest of days. Sam deserved a woman who would appreciate her as much as Brooke did. Nothing would make Brooke happier than Sam finding her happily ever after. An ache in her heart tried to tell her otherwise, but her mind stayed firmly in best friend zone.

As she got Finley ready to go to the library, his favourite place in the whole wide world, she tried to focus on her upcoming work week. She worked in project management and had a busy schedule ahead with a new project beginning for a large IT firm. She also had lunch planned with Dani on Tuesday, after receiving a confirmation text.

She had a standing weekly lunch with Sam on Wednesday, where they liked to try somewhere new each week. They had run out of places a while back and were now circling back around until somewhere new popped up, which never took long. Her heart beat a little faster as she thought about seeing Sam for lunch. What was wrong with her?

She grabbed her phone to ring Maddie, Jacob's sister, and arrange Friday night. Maddie turned twenty-one earlier this year; she was barely an adult when Jake died. She doted on Finley, and he idolized her right back, not just because she spoiled him rotten. Maddie agreed readily to mind him Friday night; she would stay over at Brooke's as she usually did, sleeping in Sam's room. Sam would just crash with Brooke. Like they'd done many times in the past.

So why did the thought suddenly make her stomach flip?

Would it be weird? No, she needed to get her head back to normal if she had any hope of not ruining their friendship. Being weird about sharing a bed wouldn't help.

Her stomach plummeted with her next thought. Would Sam even come home with her? She could end up going home with someone else. Brooke had watched Sam leave bars with other women after nights out together plenty of times in the past, but that hadn't happened since Jacob died. Not with Brooke around, at least.

Sam was a grown adult and she'd asked Brooke to be a wingwoman. It wasn't a girls' night. Sam had no obligation to stay with Brooke for the night. That was the purpose of this, right?

Thankfully, Finley pulled her out of her thoughts right then with his impatience. As she strapped him into his car seat and drove to the library, she vowed to get it out of her head. Whatever happened Friday, she would be sure to be supportive. Encouraging. The best friend that Sam had been to her all along.

If only she could get over this irrational jealousy, all would be fine.

CHAPTER FOUR

The work week finally came to an end, and Sam was both excited and apprehensive about the evening ahead. The plan was to meet Brooke at eight p.m. at Blaze, the place that would be their usual if they went out enough to have a usual. It was the only specifically queer bar in the county. Some other places had LGBTQ+ nights here and there, but this place was run by a queer couple and it was always pretty packed. They served food until late, had some pool tables and arcade games that Sam had lost many a night glued to. Neither of them were big drinkers so the relaxed atmosphere suited them well.

Sam had a couple of hours after she clocked off work to get home, change, agonize over her decision to do this, and get the bus right on time. As she walked into the bar, she looked around but couldn't see Brooke yet. Not surprising. Despite the fact that she lived close, with a toddler to wrangle, it was rare Brooke got anywhere on time. Sam was happy it was early enough to still get a booth. She grabbed a drink and sat in the one nearest the door to keep an eye out, scoping out the room as she did.

It was quiet, still early yet. There were a few familiar faces dotted around that nodded or smiled at her and some people she had never seen before. Those were the ones she was most interested in. She needed someone new, without the complications of history. A fresh start. Something she definitely wouldn't find with Brooke.

That didn't stop Sam from letting her eyes roam over Brooke's body while she made her way through the door and toward the booth. In tight denim jeans and a dark blue halter that matched her irises perfectly, she looked beautiful. Sam was in her usual black jeans and shirt, this time red, but it suited her. As Brooke sat, Sam passed her the drink she had already ordered.

"Right, what's the game plan? See anyone you like yet?" Brooke was awfully enthusiastic. Why wouldn't she be? She wanted Sam to find someone so they could go on fabulous double dates with her and whatever her name was. *Dani*. As if the name wasn't imprinted in Sam's mind. Sam took another drink before she replied, "Nobody yet, but it's early."

They chatted easily for a while, as they always did. Sam almost forgot why they were even there. It could just be another night of hanging out with her best friend, her favourite thing to do. They discussed work, Finley, a TV show they were both watching, Finley, weekend plans, and, of course, Finley. Although it was good for Brooke to get the time to herself, they both cherished him and rarely tired of discussing the funny things he said and did.

The conversation shifted to their week, although they had only met for lunch on Wednesday and knew most of the interesting things. Or so she thought.

"When I met Dani for lunch on Tuesday, she mentioned this little place we need to try for our next lunch." Brooke kept animatedly describing the place, but Sam froze. It only took Brooke a minute to know something was wrong. "What's up?" Brooke enquired, brows furrowed. "You...met Dani Tuesday?" Sam tried to sound as nonchalant as possible, but it was hard to keep the irrational hurt from her voice.

"I...yeah. I did. I thought I mentioned it."

The lie was obvious, but the reason for the lie was not. Brooke hadn't mentioned it, and she knew it. Sam could tell she knew it. Why lie? Unless...she knew Sam felt more for her and she didn't want to hurt her. That had to be it. Sam swallowed. Then she swallowed again. Brooke's eyes were anywhere but on her, and she was glad for that as she blinked back tears and excused herself to use the bathroom. She sat in the cubicle and took a minute to breathe as the familiar ache gripped her chest and her thoughts spiraled.

Brooke knew, didn't she? Of course she did.

Sam had only thought a minute ago how well they knew each other. As she ran her fingers through her hair and tried to get herself under control, her heart pounded. *Why hadn't Brooke said anything to her? But that part was obvious, wasn't it?* Sam's heart squeezed as the words she had known she would eventually have to face flitted through her mind.

Brooke thought Sam had feelings for her, and she didn't feel the same.

The pain ripped through Sam as she pressed her palm to her shaking knee. It was why Brooke insisted Dani was just a friend. Why she hadn't told her about the lunch. The easiest way to find out the truth, instead of jumping to conclusions, was to go out there and ask Brooke. Ask her best friend about this as she would about anything else. But she couldn't help but think that Brooke didn't bring it up for the same reason Sam kept her feelings to herself. Because the pain of rejection could ruin their friendship. A friendship that was much too important for that. Which meant, right now, Sam needed to pull herself together.

Nothing had changed, not really. She was still here for the same reason, possibly more so than ever. She took one more moment to remind herself she was safe, and she got her breathing under control. Then she shook it off and left the cubicle. A woman stood at the row of sinks when Sam walked out.

"Hey." The woman's voice was smooth, her smile was genuine.

"Hey." Sam was glad to see her reflection in the mirror didn't portray the spiral of minutes ago. She let her eyes wander to the woman in front of her as they both washed their hands.

She was beautiful, with warm brown skin, rich black curls that fell just past her shoulder, and startling hazel eyes that appeared to be smiling. Sam gulped. The woman didn't make a move to leave after drying her hands and neither did Sam. "Sam...me...that's my name," she stuttered and held out her hand. Like a weirdo. Did people even do that anymore? The woman didn't seem to mind. Her smile got wider as she took Sam's hand in hers, soft skin smoothly moved across her palm.

"Hi Sam, I'm Ruby."

Sam pulled her hand back reluctantly. She stood there, unsure how to proceed. Luckily, Ruby had way more skill than she did. "I better head back to my friends. Maybe I could buy you a drink later? If you're not here with someone, that is." She added that last part with a hopeful smile that sent the butterflies in Sam's stomach into overdrive. Sam marvelled at her confidence..

She usually had more skill than this, but she was never very outgoing; that's why Brooke did most of the talking when they were out with other people. Sam was always anxious about what would come out of her mouth; social situations were a minefield she hadn't quite mastered yet. "I am. I mean, here with someone. But she won't mind." Sam noticed Ruby's eyebrow rise slightly.

"Hey whatever works for you both." Sam frowned at the sentence before she replayed her own and got the meaning.

"Oh no, no, I mean not no, I don't judge but—oh God, my mouth won't cooperate with my brain's demands to shut up." Ruby laughed out loud at this and shook her head lightly.

"You're okay. Take your time. This is far better than small talk."

Sam took a breath and smiled at Ruby's words. Small talk did suck, and she'd never been any good at it. Time to try again. "I am here with someone, my friend. We're not dating. So yes, I'd love to grab a drink with you if you get bored of your friends and want to hear more barely coherent rambling."

They walked out of the bathroom together and toward where Brooke sat. As Sam pointed the booth out to Ruby, she noticed the other side was now occupied by a woman she didn't recognize. Her gut clenched at their hunched positions, deep in conversation.

Worry lines on Brooke's forehead made Sam think this wasn't a random person trying to hit on Brooke. Sam stalled a little, thinking she would just tell Ruby that her friend was busy, and they should grab that drink now. Before she got the words out, Ruby barrelled ahead of her and tapped the woman on the shoulder. "I leave you alone for one minute and you replace me? Nice, Dani."

Dani?

❖

Brooke blinked rapidly, lost for words at the person standing in front of her. Dani hadn't mentioned being here on a date. The woman laughed and quickly filled in the gaps at Brooke's obvious confusion. "Sorry, sorry. I couldn't resist. You're Brooke, right? Dani has told me a lot about you." She held her hand out to a still startled Brooke.

Brooke smiled and shook the outstretched hand, a little confused. "How'd you know my name?" Before the other woman replied, she noticed Sam approaching from her far-too-long bathroom trip. Brooke's brain and mouth had disconnected so she sighed in relief when Dani started introductions. "Brooke, this is my friend Ruby. Ruby, this is Brooke, which you seemed to have eerily guessed already. I'm assuming that the confused person standing next to you, likely wondering why her booth has been invaded, is Sam?"

As Sam registered her name, she snapped back to attention. Ruby casually placed a hand on Sam's shoulder as she spoke up. "Oh, I know Sam. We go way back. She pointed Brooke out to me, hence the name knowing." The gears in Brooke's head turned as she tried to place Ruby. She knew all of Sam's friends. She would remember a beautiful woman with charm oozing from her pores.

Sam finally found her voice, likely as shocked at the bizarre situation as Brooke was. The night had veered off course and change was not Sam's comfort. "Slight exaggeration. We just met. In the bathroom."

Sam met this woman in the bathroom, who happened to be Dani's friend? Bizarre was an understatement. She realized all eyes were on her and imagined the story that played out on her face. She tried to mask her discomfort and convey what she hoped was a picture of friendliness. "Nice to meet you, Ruby."

Sam gave her a look that said she wasn't fooling her. She wasn't doing a great job at containing the jealousy that veered its ugly head as Ruby slid into the booth and made room for Sam. Brooke explained that she'd noticed Dani at the bar when Sam left for the bathroom. Being the only queer late-night hangout in town, it was unsurprising they'd bump into each other. She left out the part where she blurted out to Dani her worries about lying to Sam and the reasons behind it that she had yet to face.

Ruby bought Sam a drink, as if she were incapable of getting her own. Brooke kept her eye roll internal this time. They chatted, all four of them. Brooke made an effort to loosen up, especially after some pointed looks from Dani and quizzical ones from Sam. Honestly, as time passed, she started to enjoy herself. Dani and Ruby were both easy to talk to. She had been right about Dani and Sam getting along. Plus, Sam saw firsthand that Brooke hadn't lied about being just friends with Dani. There were no discreet touches, no overt flirting, no gazing across at each other or under table footsie. Not between Brooke and Dani.

Ruby, on the other hand, was unabashedly doing all of those things with Sam. She worked in sales, and Brooke had no doubt she must be excellent at her job with the natural charm and confidence that shone. She even laughed at Sam's jokes and listened to the off-topic side stories with genuine enthusiasm. Sam was very clearly flattered and charmed. After one too many arm caresses, Brooke excused herself under the guise of grabbing another drink at the bar.

Dani joined her and leaned close. "You holding up okay?" Brooke sighed. Lying or pretending would be futile. Even if they'd only known each other a short amount of time, Dani was the only person who got why her head currently spun with confusion and irritation.

"I'm okay. I have no reason not to be, right? Ruby seems great." Dani took a moment before she replied. "She is. Really great. As is Sam. Actually, she looks really familiar, but I can't place her. It's been bugging me all night."

Brooke was distracted, her brain still buzzed with an overlap of confused feelings. She barely took in a word that Dani spoke.

She realized after a beat she hadn't replied. "You've probably run into each other before. It's not like it's a big place. Look, don't mention anything to Ruby about your suspicions about me and Sam okay? I don't want to ruin anything for her because I can't get my hormones under control."

Dani appeared to wrestle with her thoughts for a moment before replying. "Okay, I won't say anything unless I think it's going to hurt Ruby. But I need to warn you. Ruby's here on a mission tonight. She's not long out of a pretty shitty relationship and she's ready to hop back in the saddle, so to speak. I don't think she's exactly looking for long-term."

Brooke's chest filled with irrational anger at the idea of Ruby using Sam as her saddle, for lack of a better phrase. Sam was worth more than that. "She's most likely asking Sam to leave with her right about now. I wanted to warn you so you could try to hide that jealousy you're still denying a little better when we go back there, if Sam accepts."

Brooke appreciated the heads-up. Sam would accept. Why wouldn't she? She was here tonight for the same reason, clearly they'd hop back in that saddle together and Brooke for one did not want to bear witness to that. The mental image it brought was enough to make that ball in her chest grow spikes.

She quickly grabbed her phone and told Dani she'd meet her back at the booth as she rang Maddie to check in on Finley. He'd be fast asleep, but it was her best excuse. She needed a break before she headed back there. Watching Sam walk out the door with Ruby would shatter any pretence Brooke still maintained that her feelings were nothing more than friendly.

CHAPTER FIVE

"Finley won't settle for Maddie so I'm gonna go." Sam raised an eyebrow at Brooke's words. She was lying. Finley was down for the count by eight p.m. every night. That kid slept more than anyone she knew. Brooke looked at Sam and then pointedly darted her gaze toward Ruby, whose back was turned as she talked to Dani quietly.

Brooke was indicating that she was trying to get out of their hair. Sam's brain, heart, and libido all wrestled for attention. Ruby had just asked her not so subtly to get out of here and get to know each other better, alone. Even she wasn't out of the game long enough to not recognize code for sex. It's not like she'd never been picked up on a night out before, and she had asked Brooke to be her wingwoman tonight, right? So why did it suddenly feel so very wrong?

Dani had returned before Sam answered Ruby, and was now talking quietly to Ruby. Sam focused on Brooke. She looked sad. Sam wondered what she and Dani had discussed so intensely at the bar.

Dani and Ruby seemed finished with their conversation and Ruby's eyes were on her. Dani glanced between them all as Brooke stood, bag in hand like she was ready to flee. Sam shook her head and she could practically feel the lust-filled side of her brain scold her. "No worries, let's go wrangle the kiddo."

She turned to the two women who now regarded them curiously. "Dani, it was nice to finally meet you. Ruby, it was great chatting with you. I'm glad our bladders were in sync." Had she really just said that? The amusement on the women's faces showed her that yes, she had.

"No, Sam, honestly, stay. Enjoy the rest of your night." Brooke was restless, which was usually Sam's forte. Brooke was usually the calmer of the two.

Sam didn't hesitate with her reply. "That's all right, Brooke. I promised Fin I'd be there in the morning. I'm coming with you."

She stood her ground and Brooke had no option but to suck it up or make a scene. Sam wasn't lying. Tonight was supposed to be her chance to get back in the game. Flirt a little, dance a little, maybe even find someone who made her want to know more. But she never had any intention of falling into bed with anyone, and as tempting as Ruby made it sound, she wasn't one for breaking her promises. Finley wouldn't be happy if he woke and Sam wasn't there, ready for their day at the aquarium. It was a valid excuse, but a flimsy one. She had a feeling Brooke knew as well as she did that it was more than that.

Ruby, however, cut the conversation short and made it easy. "That's okay, we're heading off anyway. It's about past my bedtime." By the quirk of her mouth and the look in her eyes, Sam knew that was exactly where she had planned to continue their alone time. "It was great to meet you both. Maybe another time, Sam?" Her voice phrased it as a question, but she didn't wait for a reply.

She reached her hand out and squeezed Sam's as Dani said her goodbyes too. Ruby smiled at Brooke before she grabbed her bag and left them both in awe of her easy handling of the situation. Sam's eyes followed Ruby and Dani out the door as she chastised herself for not accompanying Ruby. Even if that hadn't been the plan for tonight, given what transpired before the bathroom trip, that would have been the easier option, right?

She could potentially be on her way to falling into bed with a woman who looked like she'd just walked out of a fashion magazine. Sam had no doubt, with Ruby writhing beneath her, she would forget all about the ridiculous crush she had. Even for a moment. She laughed internally at her choice of words. Crush. If only it were that simple.

As she fell into step with Brooke and they headed out, a sense of calm washed over her. It wasn't the easy option. But rarely did anything that seemed easy work out that way anyway, right? And look where stepping outside of the easy route had gotten her. Her life was full of love, adventure, and happiness. That was worth more than one night of passion. Even with someone as amazing as Ruby.

She glanced over at Brooke who seemed equally lost in her thoughts, and Sam couldn't help but think, her heart knew it was exactly where it wanted to be.

❖

"So, Finley gonna be up when we get back or magically fall asleep right in the nick of time?" Brooke rolled her eyes at Sam's teasing and knowing grin. "Shut up, Romeo. I was trying to be a good wingwoman and disappear at the right time. You're really bad at this."

Sam huffed but didn't disagree. They walked in companionable silence to Brooke's house, which wasn't far from the bar. It was a gorgeous night, a dark sky full of stars and a gentle breeze in the air.

Brooke was lost in her head. She couldn't stop thinking about the night. So much had happened in such a short amount of time. She'd almost forgotten her worry about the conversation that happened before Sam left for the bathroom and arrived back with Miss Perfect. Another mental eye roll ensued. Who finds someone in a damn bathroom? She had to admit that Ruby was great. Confident, interesting, fun. Someone she would love to be friends with under any other circumstances.

Sam had been upset that Brooke intentionally kept the lunch date with Dani from her. It seemed foolish now, trying to keep it from her in the first place. What was the point? She'd had a great time with Dani and sharing that with Sam shouldn't have been an issue. It's not like they had no other friends. Except it would've led to other conversations, including why they were just seeing each other as friends, and that wasn't a conversation Brooke was ready for. She was still figuring it out herself.

Lunch with Dani had gone even better than their first date. Without the pressure of dating, everything was so much easier. Dani had been right; they would definitely be good as friends. They'd talked, laughed, and exchanged childhood stories. Brooke had spoken about Finley quite a bit. But when she had noticed Dani at the bar, she'd almost hid. The timing was awful to introduce Dani and Sam. But on the other hand, having another person there would delay the confrontation on Brooke's lack of communication…and give her time to figure out what the heck was going on in her head. In the end, that was the deciding factor.

She had called Dani over. From the initial greeting, Dani had seemed to guess something was on Brooke's mind. Since Dani was basically the only other person who understood the reasoning behind her confusion with Sam right now, Brooke ended up quickly spilling to Dani what had just happened. She told Dani about her confused feelings about Sam trying to find someone tonight, the hurt on Sam's face when Brooke lied, for a reason she couldn't even explain to herself. The whole evening was so awkward, she'd been almost thankful to Ruby for providing a good distraction. Almost. If it hadn't been for the not-so-subtle drooling Ruby had been doing over Sam.

Brooke's internal scowl was interrupted as Sam tapped her on the shoulder, bringing her back to the present. They were home.

They walked through the door. Maddie lounged on the couch, watching some terrible reality TV show. "You're back early," she observed. "Strike out?" Sam rolled her eyes and threw a pillow from a nearby chair at her. "No, brat, I actually did pretty well for myself."

Maddie laughed. "It's not even midnight yet, Cinderella, clearly not that well." They bantered back and forth for a while as Brooke leaned against the wall and watched their verbal sparring fondly. She was used to this. Maddie had always idolized Sam. When Maddie was a teen, Sam was the cool, older girl who always paid attention to her and never made her feel like a baby. Even at times when Jake and Brooke just wanted Maddie to leave them alone, Sam always made her feel included. They joked and insulted each other like nobody's business, but they loved one another.

It was one of the many reasons Brooke loved Sam. Sam treated everyone with the same understanding and respect, regardless of what they had to offer, unless they showed they deserved otherwise. She truly cared about people and the stories they had to tell, and it showed. It was refreshing.

Brooke went upstairs to check on Finley, who was, of course, sound asleep. His dinosaur night light glowed softly and allowed a glimpse of his little face peeking out from the blanket. A mountain of stuffed toys surrounded him. She had to pinch herself sometimes when she looked at him, how absolutely perfect he was. He was the spitting image of his father with the same dark brown unruly mop of hair on his head. The same mischievous smile and charm that got him out of trouble far too often. Her heart was so full of love for him, more than she ever knew possible before he was placed in her arms the day he was born.

She shut the door again lightly, although that kid would sleep through an earthquake. Another trait inherited from Jacob. She took her time getting into pyjamas and heard Sam cross the landing as she headed to her room to do the same. Maddie came up not long after and popped her head in to say good night as Brooke got comfortable under the blanket. Sam joined her a few minutes later.

They had spent many a night lying in this very bed discussing anything and everything. Life, love, heartbreak, dreams, hopes, wishes, Finley. Of course. Tonight, however, they just lay there.

Brooke wondered if it was her imagination, or if the tension between them was palpable to Sam also.

"What were you and Dani talking about at the bar? It seemed pretty serious. Did she ask you to leave me and Ruby alone or something?" The silence was broken by Sam's soft whispers. Brooke's heart started to beat rapidly as she flashed back to the conversation. Dani had been warning her that Ruby would likely ask Sam to go back to her place. She'd wanted to prepare Brooke, in her words, so she could hide the growing jealousy if she wasn't ready to face it.

Which is why she decided to leave. She hadn't anticipated Sam leaving with her, and she wasn't sure she was ready to acknowledge how good it made her feel.

All of that was definitely not a conversation Brooke was willing to share right now, while lying in bed next to Sam. She scrambled for something to say that wasn't fully the truth, but, not quite a lie. Then she remembered something else Dani had said. "Oh, Dani was telling me you looked really familiar. She couldn't place why."

"Huh. I don't remember her. And I would. She's very beautiful." Brooke knew by Sam's mumbled voice she was already starting to doze. Sam's pinkie finger curled around Brooke's and settled her still racing heart. It was something they had done since early on, a comfort when either of them needed it. This was her way of telling Brooke that they were okay.

Brooke turned her head to face Sam. Sam's eyes were closed, but by her breathing, she wasn't asleep yet. She wrestled with whether to try to broach the conversation that spun around her head, but she wasn't sure what she would say if she tried to talk right now. She took a moment to study Sam's face and she knew her denial phase was ending. If Sam opened her eyes right now there was no way the feelings Brooke tried so hard not to feel would be concealed.

Brooke lay there as Sam started to snore softly, fingers still entwined, and tried to talk her brain out of this ridiculous state.

Sam might have found someone. She also might have blown her chances with Ruby already, in large part because of Brooke. Brooke had found someone who could have had potential and although she was happy she had a new friend, the reason it was nothing more was because her heart raced just lying here with Sam. They had both gotten a shot at happiness and keeping their friendship intact, just as it was. That's what they should be aiming for, right?

So why was Brooke's heart so heavy at the idea?

CHAPTER SIX

S am woke to an empty bed. She pried open her eyes enough to read the bedside clock and was surprised to see the digits show that she'd only been asleep a couple of hours. The cold sheets beside her indicated she'd likely been alone for most of that time, which compelled her to drag herself out of bed and find out why.

"Late night adventure?"

Sam's words sounded loud in the quiet of the night as she walked into the living room and found Brooke sitting on the couch. Sam sat next to her, worrying for a minute that Brooke was sleepwalking when she didn't receive a reply.

"We could find out."

Brooke's voice was so low Sam almost thought she imagined it, until Brooke's heated gaze met hers as Sam replied, "Find out what?"

Brooke bit her bottom lip, drawing Sam's eyes to it, then continued in a whisper so soft it barely penetrated the silence around them. "If we're compatible. We could find out."

Sam stalled. *She was joking, right?* Brooke's glance at Sam's lips while she ran her tongue over her own, said that no, she wasn't.

Before Sam knew what happened, Brooke leaned in and hesitated inches from Sam's mouth. She silently gave Sam the chance to back away. Sam leaned in almost involuntarily, and then they kissed. It started slowly as they moved together, uncertainty still lingered. That soon escalated as Brooke pushed Sam back against the couch, deepening the kiss. Tongues slipped between lips, and soft moans and sighs escaped as Sam snaked her arms around Brooke's neck, pulling her closer.

Suddenly, Sam realized what was happening. This was Brooke, her best friend for over a decade. What the hell were they doing? Brooke pulled back slightly to adjust her position and Sam took the opportunity to pause. She reluctantly pulled her hands from around Brooke and placed them on her chest.

"Wait, B, what's going on?"

Brooke's lids were heavy with lust. "We're testing a theory. Scratching an itch we both need scratched in the process. Seeing if we would be compatible, you know, ten years from now."

Sam's eyes couldn't stay off Brooke's kissable lips as her own ached for more of what they just started. *Was she dreaming?* This definitely seemed like a lot of dreams she'd been having recently. Brooke's fingers trailing up her thigh sure felt real.

Anxiety crept into her mind. She couldn't lose Brooke. She couldn't let hormones and lust ruin the best friendship she'd ever had. The best relationship of any kind, full stop. Brooke pulled back a little and cupped Sam's cheek gently. She ran her thumb against Sam's skin as Sam focused on the sensation while a sense of calm encompassed her.

"Sam. Stop panicking. It's okay. We don't have to do anything you're not okay with."

Sam lifted her gaze to Brooke's eyes. There was no fear behind them as Brooke stared back at Sam. Despite the calming touch, Sam couldn't fully shake the worry. She needed to get it out.

"I can't lose you too, Brooke."

Brooke reached out and grasped Sam's hand where it lay on her thigh. "Nothing in the world would make that happen. But we can absolutely forget I said a thing. I don't want anything that you don't want, Sam."

Sam couldn't process anything except the body so close to her. Heat radiated across her skin. Her eyes landed back on the mouth she would spend many nights dreaming of. This could be the worst decision of her life, but as she looked at Brooke and listened to her soothing voice, Sam knew she was safe. Safe, and very, very turned on.

She skipped words and pressed her body against Brooke's as she moulded their lips together again. Brooke hesitated, so Sam linked their pinkie fingers together. A promise that everything was okay. Brooke let go and kissed her with nothing held back.

Her last thought before she forced her brain to shut up was that she was kissing her best friend as if her life depended on it and damn if right then it didn't feel like it just might.

❖

Brooke grabbed Sam's hand and pulled her toward the bedroom. The room she'd had to leave a couple of hours earlier to stop herself from waking Sam to do exactly what they were doing now. They had been kissing for both a moment and an eternity all at the same time and Brooke was lost in a haze of lust. They stopped to kiss along the way, and she couldn't help but wonder how they'd never done this before because damn it was good.

She didn't have time to dwell on it as they entered her bedroom. After clicking the lock shut on the door, Sam pushed her onto her four-poster bed and wasted no time before climbing on top of her to resume their kiss. Brooke tugged at Sam's night shirt until Sam sat back and pulled it over her head. Brooke's mouth went dry as the thin material fell to the floor. It left her full, perfect breasts on display.

Brooke reached up and ran a thumb over one of Sam's puckered nipples. Her heart rate increased as Sam's head fell back, and she arched into the touch. Brooke needed her mouth where her thumb currently resided. She pulled Sam down and took one nipple into her mouth, circling it with her tongue before sucking. Sam's hand landed on the back of her head and gripped her hair as Brooke paid careful attention to the hardened pebble between her teeth.

Sam's moans only added fuel to the already consuming fire. Desire curled in Brooke's stomach, and she was close to the edge already. Sam hadn't even touched her yet. She paid the same attention to the other nipple, slowly working her tongue around in circles as Sam pressed down against her thigh hard.

Sam pulled back and stood to pull off her pyjama pants and lacy, black underwear while Brooke watched hungrily. Her body was perfect. With fair white skin peppered with light freckles, curves in all the right places, and confidence to match, Sam was simply gorgeous.

Brooke took a moment to wonder how she had gone so long without paying attention to this. She was certainly aware now. She took in every detail greedily, memorizing the dips and curves she'd seen so many times yet never allowed herself to appreciate.

Sam reached down to tug at Brooke's pants. "You're overdressed," she stated, her eyes eager. Since her brief earlier hesitation, Sam had gained a confidence that, from their many late-night conversations, Brooke knew she always held in the bedroom. Something Brooke never expected to experience firsthand. Sam was in control, and Brooke was definitely okay with that.

Brooke slowly removed her T-shirt; old self-conscious thoughts flew through her brain with each layer shed. It had been so long since she had someone really pay attention to her naked body. Although her comfort in her own skin had grown over the years, she was definitely not as confident as Sam in her body.

As her T-shirt dropped to the floor, her eyes didn't quite meet Sam's. Sam stopped her movements. "Is this okay?"

Sam's voice was calm and kind. Brooke recognized Sam was worried she was having second thoughts.

"Yes...I want this. I definitely want this. It's just been a while since anyone has seen me like this and after having a kid, everything isn't exactly, well..." She gestured at Sam's body still hovering above her. "Like that."

Sam put her finger under Brooke's chin and lifted her head to meet her eyes. Brooke's breath left her body at the absolute lust and appreciation reflected back at her. "You're beautiful."

And under Sam's gaze, Brooke believed it. Brooke wondered at Sam's ability to always make her feel so damn special. It was one of the things that made Brooke determined to keep Sam in her life all those years ago. Sam had a way of making Brooke love so many parts of herself she never fully appreciated before.

Brooke removed her pants with growing enthusiasm. Once she lay there in just her underwear, Sam took over. She peeled the fabric slowly down Brooke's thighs and bit her lip, the ache between Brooke's legs intensifying.

Brooke reached up and pulled Sam on top of her, unable to wait any longer. They kissed again, slower this time as their hands started to explore previously unknown territories.

As Sam's hand trailed between her legs, Brooke knew she wouldn't last very long. "Sam, I…"

Sam kissed her, smothering her strangled words, and smiled as she worked her fingers faster against her. "Just let go," she whispered.

That was all it took.

Within seconds, Brooke tumbled over the edge, and moans escaped as her legs shook. The indescribable pleasure that coursed through her body was amplified as Sam held her close through the aftershocks, her movements slowing as she kissed her softly.

Before she even finished shaking, Sam peppered kisses down her body and positioned herself between her legs. As Sam's tongue dipped inside her already sensitive core, she arched against her mouth, and her hands found their way into Sam's hair.

Sam was an expert. There was no other explanation for the sensations Brooke currently experienced. She rarely came that quickly, never mind twice in a row, but she was already climbing again as Sam kissed and licked and sucked all the right places.

"Sam—" Her voice cracked as she was ready to explode. Sam's tongue dipped in and out quickly and then she moved to suck exactly where Brooke needed. A release even bigger and longer than the last rocked through her body.

Sam slowed her kisses before she rested her head against Brooke's thigh. She appeared to be getting her own breathing under control. Brooke tugged on Sam's arm, to pull her up toward her. She held Sam close and they kissed slowly as her body recovered. Sam pulled back and smiled as her fingers moved across Brooke's cheek almost instinctively.

Brooke's heart flipped; butterflies that hadn't appeared in far too long took up residence in her stomach. She kissed Sam again deeply as she let her hands wander down Sam's sweat-slickened skin.

"Brooke, you don't—"

She shut Sam up with a moan as her fingers found their goal. Brooke might not have had as much experience as Sam in the bedroom when it came to women, but this wasn't her first time. It had been a long time since her one and only college girlfriend, and even longer since she discovered her attraction wasn't limited to boys, but with Sam's body beneath her fingertips she didn't feel in the least out of her depth.

Brooke kissed a path down Sam's body and circled her tongue around where Sam needed her most. She pushed two fingers inside and was met with a whimper as Sam arched against her. She moved her fingers faster as she licked and sucked and Sam's legs clenched around her head.

She could get lost in Sam if she let herself, she was sure of it.

As Sam tumbled into bliss, Brooke slowed her movements and kissed her way back up Sam's beautiful body to collapse beside her. Her breaths still laboured, she reached out and held Sam's hand.

As the fog of lust started to clear, all the reasons why she had left the bed in the first place came screeching back. Would tonight be a one-time deal? They were best friends, and they couldn't put that in jeopardy, not for anything. As much as she told Sam nothing would change, they had to be careful. Why jeopardize a friendship as special as theirs just for orgasms? Even if they were amazing, mind-blowing orgasms. She looked at Sam, who stared at her with undeniable lust. Her body reacted almost immediately and moved toward Sam again. If all they got was one night, she planned to make it a long one.

CHAPTER SEVEN

The next morning, Sam woke to Finley's weight landing on her with a thud. She pried open one eye, which revealed his giggling face hovering above hers. She was thankful they'd had enough awareness to throw pyjamas on before falling asleep in the early hours of the morning. She peered to the right and blinked to clear her sleep-addled brain as she took in Brooke's smile aimed at her. She smiled back, her heart fluttering as she allowed herself a moment to admire the view before she tuned in to what the bouncing three-year-old was saying.

"It's aquarium day, Sammy, get up!"

She narrowed her eyes at the alarm clock on the bedside locker. Eight o'clock glowed softly from the backlit screen. By some miracle, Finley had let them sleep in a bit. Which was well needed, considering the time they actually untangled themselves to get some sleep. She grabbed Finley and tickled him mercilessly, his squeals of laughter the perfect morning sound. He flopped down into the bed between them, his head turning from one to the other.

"Story!"

Sam smiled at his melodic tone, and she settled in to listen as Brooke proceeded to tell one of his favourite stories, the tale of how they met. Sam's mind started to drift back ten years. Memories of how closed off she was from the world and everyone in it flitted through her mind. That was, until Brooke came along. She half paid attention to Brooke's dramatized, kid-friendly version of events as she reminisced.

Sam was struggling to stay awake during class when she heard the words she dreaded come from the lecturer's mouth: group assignment. Her eyes popped open as her heart began to race. She had acquaintances in college, people she said hello to or sat next to in the cafeteria occasionally. But she had no friends, and that was by design. In her limited experience, friends were never a good idea.

Group projects meant lots of time spent with other people. As her classmates began to sort into groups, she hoped to be overlooked and have to do it alone. A girl across the room caught her eye and beckoned her over, killing that dream. As she studied the girl, she found herself going. Whether it was because of the killer smile or just out of fear of being rude, she didn't know.

"Hey, I'm Brooke. This is Liam. You looked like you could use a group, and we could use a third."

Yeah, it was definitely the smile. The bubbly personality attached to it was far from Sam's comfort zone, but she found herself drawn to Brooke. That's how she ended up roped into a group of three, although Liam seemed more interested in Brooke than the project. Sam didn't blame him.

As classes went on, Brooke showed no interest in him and Sam noticed her discomfort growing at his persistence. When Sam took it upon herself to make it impossible for him to pester Brooke, he soon gave up joining their sessions altogether. That left her and Brooke, which was fine by Sam. She quickly started looking forward to their meetups.

Sam knew she was gay. The realization struck while living in a group home when her best friend at the time kissed her and promptly broke her heart. They had a short but intense romance until six weeks later, Kira left for a foster home, and Sam never saw her again. Which solidified Sam's thinking that friendship, or any form of relationship, sucked. Not knowing what rejection sensitive dysphoria was back then, all Sam knew was love equalled rejection. And rejection? That equalled pain.

But it meant she understood her instant attraction to Brooke for the crush it was. Sam allowed herself to enjoy the fleeting feelings for the length of the project. A couple of weeks later, it became significantly easier to ignore her crush when Brooke introduced Sam to her boyfriend, Jacob. They had been dating for a few months. Sam realized that the late nights working over pizza, early morning coffee, and now an introduction to the boyfriend were getting scarily close to friendship level.

When she told Brooke she had ADHD in a rambled stream of words to try to explain why she had yet again forgotten her project notes, she figured that would be the end of that. She waited for the usual responses. The ones she'd heard most of her life about how it was no excuse or how she should try harder or the all too common "isn't that just boys." Even the few people who had tried to be understanding by saying, "everybody forgets sometimes," eventually realized that "sometimes" was a daily thing. Sam hated seeing the disappointment eventually appear on their faces. That's why she had gotten used to being the one to leave before she was left.

However, Brooke's reaction was complete and utter acceptance. Not even a hint of judgment or scepticism passed Brooke's lips. Her only question was to ask Sam how she could help. Of course, asking for help was something Sam had learned not to do very early on, so even then, she shrugged it off and made a self-deprecating joke. She soon learned Brooke wasn't so easily swayed.

Brooke was patient. She helped Sam manage her time for the project and kept her on track without Sam having to ask. Brooke was positive and motivating and, for the first time Sam could remember, she not only finished a project on time, they got it completed early.

That level of support was not something Sam was used to, and it both calmed and terrified her. She felt safe around Brooke.

Safe to be exactly who she was. Except she still had no clue what that meant, and the feelings creeping up on her sent off warning signals in her brain. Brooke could mean something to her. If Sam were honest, in the short amount of time they'd known each other, she already did. In Sam's experience, caring about someone eventually led to losing them. If it already hurt to think about not seeing Brooke for their study sessions, how would it feel when Brooke eventually got sick of her?

So, Sam did what she always did. Once the project was submitted, she began to withdraw. Her fight-or-flight kicked in at even the chance of facing rejection from Brooke and...she flew. She ignored Brooke's attempts to meet up, she didn't see her outside of class and answered any messages with the bare minimum. Luckily for her, Brooke wasn't easily ignored. She didn't give up.

One day, Sam was sitting in her dorm room when there was a knock on the door. Opening it, she found Brooke standing with Sam's favourite pizza and beer along with that endearing smile. She rambled about wanting to spend time with Sam. She gave Sam an opening for a clean slate. No judgment, no questions asked.

Sam stood at the door, mouth open in shock. Nobody had ever gone to lengths like this simply to spend time with her. It was one of the first times she ever remembered feeling like someone wanted her in their life. Before she talked herself out of it, she moved aside for Brooke to walk in.

Although her instincts to protect herself never disappeared, Brooke made it easier day by day for Sam to believe she didn't need to. Letting Brooke into her life was a decision Sam never regretted. Or, as Brooke told it to Finley in the light-hearted, fairy-tale version he adored, she didn't give Sam a choice.

Finley giggled at that part, as he always did, and Sam snapped out of her trip down memory lane. She looked across at Brooke and her heart flipped as that same killer smile was shot her way. Over ten years later, and the whirlwind had never ceased.

Brooke had upended Sam's life in the best possible way and continued to do so every day since.

❖

Later that day, they walked through the doors of the aquarium, and Finley's eyes lit up. He pulled his hands from Brooke's and Sam's and ran straight to the circular fish tank in the middle of the room filled with every colour fish imaginable.

Sam smiled; she loved days like this when it was just the three of them. Finley's excitement grew by the minute. Brooke kept glancing at her as if to make sure she was witnessing all the silly things he did. It was all so normal. Just a regular family day out.

When they got to the shark tank, Fin set up camp in front of it, legs crossed as he sat on the floor in awe. Sam and Brooke settled into the chairs at the edge of the room, knowing they'd be here a while.

"So...did you get Ruby's number last night?"

Sam was startled at Brooke's question. She recalled in vivid detail what happened after they got home, and confusion hit as she wondered why Brooke was talking about Ruby. If last night really was just a one-time thing, scratching an itch as Brooke had said, then Brooke's attempt at normal conversation sucked. But now wasn't the time to get into that. "I did not. As you kindly pointed out, my skills need polishing."

"They really do. You suck at this." Brooke stuck out her tongue mocking Sam, but what the action sparked in Sam was far more than humour.

"Got you into bed, didn't I?"

Brooke's mouth dropped open and Sam's face filled with heat at her own words. This was one of those moments where Sam didn't even hear the sentence before it left her mouth. Humour was always her go-to for fixing things, but fearing she might have gone too far this time, she found a sudden fascination with the ground.

Before Sam could resort to using Finley as a barrier, Brooke broke the silence with laughter as she shoved her shoulder lightly. "Technically, I got you into bed, but I'll let your ego take this one."

Sam was thankful for the ease that remained between them, despite their far from friend-like escapades. "How're things with Dani going? You seemed to get on well last night."

Brooke fidgeted beside her before answering.

"Good, actually. She's definitely someone I can see being a good friend. She invited me to go to an art exhibition on Friday."

Sam frowned. "What about Fin?"

Brooke's eyes darted around, and a bad feeling crept into Sam's gut. "I asked Maddie before she left this morning. I didn't want you to feel obligated in case, you know, you want to make plans with Ruby or someone."

Sam's heart sank as the familiar ache began. This was it, right? It had started already. Brooke was beginning to treat her differently. She always asked Sam first; it was their unspoken rule. There was nothing wrong with Maddie minding Finley; he loved her. But Sam was the first pick for Fin duties, always. Until this morning.

She perched silently on the edge of her chair, not even sure what to say. Her voice would convey her hurt if she even tried, so she kept quiet.

"Sam, I—"

Finley chose that moment to run over and drag Sam to see something the stingray was doing in the nearby tank. She held his hand tightly, and her heart fractured just a little bit. She couldn't imagine her life without him. She couldn't imagine loving him more if he were her own. What would happen if she didn't get these feelings under control, so Brooke didn't tiptoe around her?

Right then, her phone went off in her pocket. One new message from Maddie.

Are you busy Friday? Brooke said you might have plans but if not, wanna eat way too much sugar and watch sappy movies when little dude goes to bed? Carl is on night shift.

Sam smiled softly. It was funny how people came into your life and ended up meaning so much, especially for someone like Sam who hadn't known that for so long. Jacob's whole family had enveloped her in so much love that it wasn't even feasible to attempt her walls up technique.

Part of her understood she had overreacted. Her brain was miles ahead, already anticipating the end of the longest relationship she'd ever had in her life. She hadn't even had time to really process last night, but losing Brooke in any capacity was enough to send her spiralling. Logically, she reminded herself what seemed like rejection was really just Brooke looking out for her and trying to give her space to find the relationship Sam said she wanted. Except the last thing she wanted from Brooke was space. Why did everything have to be so complicated?

She sent off a quick reply to Maddie in agreement as Brooke came to join them. It didn't need to be so complicated. She would hang out with Maddie, talk too much, eat too much and not think about Brooke out with another woman. Because that thought sparked a whole new level of fear, even if it really did appear that they were just friends.

Brooke took Finley's hand, and the three of them continued their journey through the aquarium. They didn't speak any more about the non-date. Or about last night. In fact, they barely spoke at all unless it was to Finley. What was happening to them? Was one night, however amazing it had been, really worth this?

Sam was off kilter all day. They rarely fought, but when they did, nothing was right in Sam's world. This wasn't even a fight really, but she couldn't shake the idea that this was the start of a big change. Why did she have to be so awkward all the time? Why couldn't she just ignore her feelings like a regular human being and live a life of secretly lusting after her best friend in peace? She had been fine doing that for years.

She'd barely registered her feelings when Jake was around, and even after, when they spent more time together than ever before. But since last night when she'd finally gotten to know what it was like to have Brooke beneath her, she knew it wasn't going to be as easy to switch it off again. Still, she couldn't find it in her heart to regret the night that she knew would play on repeat in her head while she was alone. It was a good, hot memory. And, if their current awkwardness was anything to go by, a memory was how it had to stay.

When they finished up after the final tank, they went to the café in the lobby for ice cream. Finley was super excited about this part of the day. Ice cream was his absolute favourite—mint chocolate chip, just like Sam. They sat down outside in the sun, and Sam had never been so thankful for Finley's chatter in her life. Otherwise, the silence would have been deafening.

Finally, sick of it, she just sighed. "This is ridiculous."

Brooke looked at her, nodding, as she watched Finley run off to the play area close by. "I'm sorry I didn't ask you to mind Finley. I should have asked you first."

Brooke paused, but Sam cut in before she continued. "No, I'm sorry. You were thinking of me. You didn't want to put me under pressure. It was likely if someone asked me out, I would say no if I agreed to mind Finley. I was just hurt initially. But I understand."

"I just…I don't want to hold you back, Sam. You've given so much. Time, energy, everything. You've been a constant for me and Fin and I will forever be thankful for that. But you need to put you first too."

Sam grappled with what to say. The thoughts tumbling around her head were too jumbled to make sense of, and she worried that opening the floodgates of how she actually felt would unravel something she wasn't ready to face.

"I don't want things to change between us. Not in the way they have today, anyway. I don't want us walking on eggshells around each other. You and Fin mean the world to me."

Sam bit her lip after she spoke, so many more words fighting to find their way out. Brooke looked like she was hesitating with what to reply but, in the end, she just smiled softly.

"We suck at being annoyed with each other."

"We really do. Let's just not bother. Deal?" Sam held out her pinkie finger and Brooke quickly linked hers.

"Deal. Look at us being all grown up and communicating and stuff."

A weight lifted from Sam and the drive back to Brooke's held a significantly lighter mood. There was much more to it than what they had discussed. But she was content to leave it be. They were okay, and that's all that mattered.

❖

Brooke sat back in her office chair and placed her phone on the desk. She had been texting Dani to find out what to wear on Friday. Classy but comfortable was not a helpful reply in the slightest.

If they were dating, then this would be their third date. Were third dates still when sex was on the cards? Brooke didn't know the etiquette anymore. She and Jake began dating in college, so it wasn't exactly regular rules. She was suddenly thankful to Dani for saving her the worry. She wasn't sure she was ready for sex. At least not with anyone she wasn't comfortable with.

Her body had been through a lot since the last time she really tried to impress someone. A baby, breastfeeding, motherhood in general. Plus, copious amounts of chocolate and ice cream to get her through the grief and late nights. She wasn't ashamed of her body, but she certainly didn't look the same as she had in college. That was something she had to figure out how to be okay with.

Plus, if she did eventually date someone, how did it even happen? She wouldn't bring anyone back to her house so soon, not with Finley there. That would mean she'd have to go to their place. Or would they end up doing it in the car? God no, that was for teenagers, right?

Her stomach filled with butterflies right as her heart clenched at the thought. She hadn't been with anyone since Jake until the night with Sam. One person for over a decade and then her best friend. Sam seemed more than happy, but she didn't think that counted. They were uniquely in tune with each other. She had slept with one woman before Jake, so it wasn't that she was totally new to it, but she was young at the time and inexperienced.

Her phone rang, and she jumped. She had been in a daze, the emails on her laptop having been neglected for far too long. She sat up and answered her phone.

"We're still on for lunch at one?" It was Sam. Obviously it was Sam, they had lunch together every Wednesday. Which she had forgotten. She was the worst. She couldn't cancel, not with the weirdness between them recently.

"I've had a manic morning. How do you feel about bringing me lunch here and chatting while I catch up on emails? Pretty please?"

"Sure. I'll be by in about an hour."

They both worked in the city which was helpful. Although, nowhere was particularly far from anywhere around here. It was both a blessing and a curse at times. After they hung up, Brooke tackled her ever-increasing mailbox. Before she knew it, her office door opened, and Sam was there. Brooke held up one finger, finishing her email. When she looked up, Sam had set up their sandwiches, her favourite from the deli close to Sam's office. Her mouth watered at the sight.

"You are the best."

Sam nodded her acknowledgement. "Yes, yes I am. Keep typing."

Brooke continued, taking breaks to eat and chat about everything and nothing. It was comfortable, thankfully. That is until she had to go and open her awkward mouth.

"Has sex changed?"

She froze as soon as the words left her lips. She didn't even know what she was going to say until it was out. She swallowed, wishing the ground would do the same to her. They were just getting back to normal, and she decided that this was the best topic of conversation?

Sam tilted her head and the smirk on her face made Brooke's cheeks heat as Sam replied, "I think you need to elaborate."

"Forget I said anything. That was weird." Brooke turned back to her laptop, cheeks ablaze.

"Hold up, you're not getting off that lightly. If best friends can't talk about sex, what can they talk about? It's not like we haven't before. So, spill. What's going on?"

Sam seemed relaxed. And she was right, they never had a problem talking about this stuff before. Brooke was making it weird again. "Well, I was just thinking it's been so long since I've dated, I don't know the etiquette anymore. Is date three still the sex date? What do people even do these days? Is everyone kinky? It was just Jake for over ten years. Then me, myself, and I since then. Until, well, us. But that wasn't planned, and I wasn't freaking out. I'm out of my depth."

Brooke barely took a breath between sentences. If she didn't get it all out, she'd lose her nerve. Sam looked at her for a moment as her grin still lingered, before finally putting her out of her misery. "Okay, I'm gonna try to remember what you said but it was a lot, so bear with me. Sex hasn't changed. Everyone is different, which you know. Yes, everyone is kinky now, the internet has done fabulous things."

She laughed at Brooke's wide-eyed look. "Seriously, Brooke, relax. Date three doesn't have to be the sex date unless you want it to be. Do what feels right to you."

Sam hesitated a moment and Brooke almost filled the silence, but then she continued. "Dani would be a very lucky girl to get to be with you, so remember that and don't do anything you aren't comfortable with. And for the record, you're still more than capable."

Brooke stared at Sam before her words registered and Brooke realized her mistake. "No, no. Not Dani. We really are just friends. My thoughts just got out of hand and I was thinking about future dating scenarios and—" She dropped her head into her arms before mumbling more, "I just wish I didn't have to go through this whole *new to each other* thing. Can't someone just know what I like, and vice versa, and be done with it already?"

A frown formed on Sam's face as she shook her head. "Brooke, the *new to each other* thing is the best part. Finding out what makes the other person sigh in a certain way. What places make them shudder when you kiss. What makes them melt in your arms. Hearing your name on their lips for the very first time. That's the best feeling."

Brooke hadn't realized she was staring until Sam gulped. Their eyes locked, and Brooke couldn't pull hers away. Images flashed into her mind all at once. Sam beneath her, moaning as Brooke ran her tongue along her neck. Her body writhing as Brooke moved her fingers between Sam's legs. Her name being called as she brought Sam to the edge of bliss and watched her tumble over.

"Brooke?" Sam's whispered word took a moment to enter her brain. Brooke shook the thoughts from her head, and her cheeks flamed. Oh, God, what was wrong with her? She cleared her throat and found her voice, hoping it wasn't shaking as badly as her legs concealed under the desk.

"You make it all sound so easy." If Sam noticed the slight huskiness to her voice, she ignored it.

"Sometimes it's easy, sometimes it's not. But is it worth it? With the right person, or even a super-hot wrong one—totally." Sam's grin lightened the mood. Brooke laughed. She missed joking with her best friend.

"Seriously, Brooke, just chill. When the time comes, take it slowly. Don't rush into anything just because you feel like you should, but don't hold back out of fear or guilt. Jake would want you to be happy."

Brooke nodded. The emotion that coated her throat appeared out of nowhere. Sam was right, but it didn't make it easier to hear. Sam got up, walked around the desk, and took her hand. She wiped a stray tear that had escaped from Brooke's eye.

"He would want you to be happy. That's all he ever wanted. And so do I. You deserve it, Brooke. You make everyone else so happy; it's about time you put yourself first."

Brooke stared up at Sam, the second most important person in her life. The feel of Sam's thumb as it caressed her fingers sent shivers up her arm as she saw the truth behind every single word in Sam's eyes. She wanted Brooke to be happy. But Brooke was already happy. Finley and Sam made sure of that. They were her happiness.

Where did a new person fit into all of this? Could they be part of her happiness? Could someone else fit in with the family they had created? Did Brooke even want them to? Her mind flashed back to lying in bed last night next to Sam and the thoughts and subsequent dreams that had followed. She knew the answers. But she wasn't ready to take that risk yet, even if the woman in front of her made happiness seem like a given.

The rest of lunch went by quickly as they returned to lighter topics. After Sam left, their conversation played in Brooke's head on repeat. Jake would want her to be happy. She knew that without a doubt. Just as she never questioned that Sam wanted her to be happy.

Her heart squeezed as she remembered earlier inappropriate thoughts. For a brief moment, she allowed herself to imagine how much happier they could be. One moment, before she shut down that thought.

It was a risk she couldn't take. Finley and Sam were her family; she couldn't put that in jeopardy. Even for a chance at more. She closed her eyes and images of Sam's lips inches from hers popped into her head.

She was in trouble.

CHAPTER EIGHT

"They should just both ditch him and get with each other. Do you see their chemistry?" Sam pointed vehemently at the screen as Maddie shook her head in amusement.

"You say that about every rom-com we watch."

Sam grabbed a handful of popcorn from the bowl between them before she replied. "Listen, it's not my fault that every leading lady they cast has more chemistry with the other women than with the Prince Charming dude who is really just a mediocre white guy." Maddie scoffed but Sam knew she agreed with her on this one. This movie sucked big time.

It might have something to do with the fact that she was only half paying attention. The other half of her mind was focused on how Brooke's *not a date* date was going. She'd been less than subtle when Brooke walked down the stairs earlier. The above the knee cocktail dress Brooke wore, with her chocolate brown curls dancing right above the V dip that led Sam's eyes directly to the cleavage on display made Sam's almost drooling hard to hide.

After they got the kiddo to sleep, Sam and Maddie made popcorn and gathered way too many sugary snacks to begin their rom-com marathon, of which they were already nearing the end of movie number two. Who thought this was a good distraction technique? How had she not ever realized exactly how many rom-coms centred around friends ignoring not so friend-like feelings?

"You must relate to that." Maddie's words registered a beat later as Sam realized she'd zoned out. She froze as she replayed them in her head. Relate? Why would she relate? What did Maddie suspect? Her heart thumped in her chest as she opened and closed her mouth.

"Sorry, maybe that was a touchy subject to bring up. I just meant…I mean…it must be hard not knowing any of your family."

Sam was sure the confusion was written all over her face until she properly paid attention to the screen in front of them. The main character, a high-powered businesswoman who apparently loved money more than anything in the world, was finally opening up about her lack of family and her abandonment issues. Ah yes. That, she certainly related to. She figured Maddie was probably trying to figure out how to time travel back a few minutes, so she connected her brain to her mouth and put her out of her misery.

"Yeah, I mean, I didn't get the ruthless money hoarding side, but I certainly get the fear of abandonment being so strong you want to shut all of the emotions off completely. It was very much like that for me, before."

"Before…" Maddie let the sentence hang and Sam filled it in before she even thought about it.

"Before Brooke." It was true. It was true in every sense of the word. Before Brooke, the idea of anyone meaning so much to her that she could not imagine a life without them was terrifying. Because nobody lasted. Nobody stayed. Nobody was worth that kind of pain. Before Brooke.

Now she had two people who meant as much to her as she imagined any blood relative would, and a whole bunch of people, including Maddie, who she considered family. Maddie was quiet for a bit as Sam got lost in her thoughts before she spoke again.

"Did you ever try to find them? Your family?" It wasn't a new question. She'd been asked it a few times over the years when people found out she was a foster kid and didn't know anyone she was related to.

"No, I didn't. I read through some of my social work files once I was old enough, the ones they could still get a hold of that is, so I know who they are. Or who they were, at least. But no. I've never looked."

"Why? Weren't you curious? I'm not sure I could stop myself."

Sam sighed. She wasn't upset with Maddie for asking about it. She could shut down the conversation in a second and Maddie wouldn't push. It's just one of those things that she found so hard to explain outside of her head, so she never tried. People had this picture in their minds of an Annie-style happy ending, or of her sitting on a windowsill wishing for parents to come and help her find a home. That was the dream for most kids, right? But her brain wasn't that kind. Or naive. Even as a child.

Sam wasn't sure if it was the rom-com, the sugar, or Maddie's silence, that allowed her to gather her thoughts. Whatever it was, for probably the first time, she was honest about it.

"Yeah. I was curious, of course I was, and still am. There were plenty of times I had a search engine up and their names typed in, or I stopped myself from typing them into social media. Part of me craves knowing what they are like now. But that part is completely overshadowed by the other part of me that never wants to feel the way I still remember feeling every time a foster family decided I was too much work. Every time they used my ADHD diagnosis as an excuse to label me difficult and request a change of placement. It took so much unpacking to realize that I was never the problem, and I still work hard to remind myself of that. I just picture seeing photos of my parents plastered on social media. Happy. With kids, ones they chose to keep. Ones they tried hard enough for. Ones they wanted. I'm not sure how I'd get past that."

She wasn't exactly sure when the tears had started to fall, but she wiped them away quickly and shrugged as Maddie reached out a hand and placed it on her arm.

"Maybe if I had tried harder, I could've gotten adopted by a rich dude and worn a pretty red dress and all would be right with the world. Let me tell you, that would still be a better movie than this one."

Maddie squeezed Sam's arm and pity laughed before replying. "If you ever need to talk about it, I'm here, okay? I know you've got Brooke and she loves you. But I know she has a tendency to want to find solutions, especially because she cares about you so much, and sometimes you just need to feel how you feel. If you need to get some of this shit out, I'm a good listener."

"You are. I'll keep that in mind." Sam meant it. She appreciated it. Maddie was right, Brooke was her best friend, but if Sam told her this, Brooke would want to fix it. She would want Sam to move past this. She would want to help her find her family if she thought that's what Sam wanted. Maybe it was. But Sam wasn't ready for that.

Someday she might be but right now, the fear of rejection was far greater than the curiosity.

❖

As Brooke and Dani walked through the doors of the community centre where the exhibition was being held, Brooke instantly relaxed. They had gone to dinner first, where Dani promised her that it was a casual event, and you didn't need to know anything about art to appreciate it. But Brooke had remained sceptical. The most she knew about art was the colourful scribbled drawings taped to her fridge. From Finley—and Sam. She smiled to herself as she pictured both their heads stuck together, Sam just as enthusiastic about her masterpieces as Fin.

When she envisioned an art exhibition, she pictured a large gallery with wine and cheese being served by waiters in penguin suits, while attractive, fashionable people discussed the meaning behind pictures that to her looked like random shapes or splotches. However, if anything, Brooke was probably a little overdressed. Soft, chill music played in the background. The crowd, quite large for the size of the space, were a mixed bunch. Some, like her, in dresses and heels. Others, in jeans and T-shirts. Some sat around on couches or bean bags chatting, while others walked around looking at the pieces on display.

Brooke followed Dani's lead as she headed to the right of where they entered. There wasn't an obvious flow to the artwork, or at least not one she easily distinguished, so people hopped around to whatever caught their eye. She was happy to let Dani show her the way for this. Dani was immediately absorbed. It was easy to see her passion as she talked to Brooke about the various pieces they looked at. She knew most of the artists, some personally, some by name. The exhibition was a charity event to raise money for a local community youth program, so a lot of the work on display was by teenagers involved in the program and their tutors.

Brooke kept an eye out for something to buy. She was happy to support the centre and even happier that the art was actually very good. She thought she might struggle to pick something she would like, but the opposite was true. She couldn't narrow it down. They reached a piece that caught her eye and she stopped. The image was striking. It was an ocean hitting off rocks, the clouds dark and looming above. What was most striking were two figures off to the right, seemingly under a ray of sunshine, protected from the chaos surrounding them. It was breathtaking. Calm within a storm. She glanced at the artist's name, A. Lynch.

She glanced around and couldn't see a sold sticker yet.

Dani's eyes were on her when she turned. "Beautiful, isn't it?"

"Yeah. Do you know the artist? I'd love to buy it before someone else does." Dani looked at the name and frowned. Her eyebrows furrowed as she appeared to try to recall the name before she exclaimed, "That's it!"

Brooke wondered if she had missed something. "That's... what?"

"That's why I thought Sam looked so familiar."

Relief was evident in Dani's exclamation, but Brooke was still confused. Even more so when Dani took her hand and led her toward the opposite side of the room, away from the painting she hoped nobody would snatch up before she figured out what exactly Dani was talking about.

"It wasn't that I had seen Sam before. It was Lexi. The artist you were asking about. I've only ever seen her a few times in passing or when I was volunteering at the centre, so that's why it didn't click right away. But the resemblance is uncanny."

Dani's destination became apparent when she stopped near a group of people at the front of the hall and tapped someone on the shoulder. Dani started to speak as the person turned around and Brooke blinked once, twice, and a third time just to be sure her eyes weren't playing tricks on her.

"Lexi, good to see you again. My friend here is interested in buying one of your pieces, so I figured I would introduce you. This is Brooke."

The young woman smiled at her and Brooke knew that was her cue. A smile that resembled one she was intimately familiar with. It was like looking at Sam, the first time they met in college. She shook out of it as the woman, Lexi, talked to her about the painting. Brooke agreed to the price, barely registering what was said and was lost in her thoughts as Dani chatted with Lexi for a few minutes about the centre and the exhibition.

As Lexi got pulled away a few minutes later by another wannabe customer, Dani whispered. "I was right, wasn't I? It's uncanny." Brooke nodded, still trying to catch up to her thoughts and their meaning. It was weird for sure. But, these things happened, right? She'd heard it plenty of times. People being mistaken for other people. Having lookalikes out there running around. It didn't mean anything, it was just some weird coincidence.

Dani spoke up again while they continued through the exhibition, as Brooke glanced around to look for Lexi more than the art they were here to see.

"It's funny that that's the painting you picked. Seems Sam's got a long-lost sister floating around, eh?" Dani laughed at her own comment as one thought flitted around Brooke's head.

That's exactly how it appeared.

CHAPTER NINE

Sammy, why do you not have any chocolate on your pancakes?" Sam looked over at Finley's syrup-covered face. He clearly couldn't fathom anyone not wanting to slather their food with excessive amounts of sugar if it was an option.

"I prefer butter, Fin. Just like you prefer jam on your toast." Finley nodded his acceptance of the answer and continued to layer his pancakes. Sam didn't have the heart to stop him.

She had picked Finley up from his grandparents for their Sunday date because Brooke claimed to have a last-minute work meeting for a demanding client. Sam half wondered if it had been an excuse to avoid her. She wasn't quite sure what was going on with Brooke, but something was definitely off.

After their slightly intense lunch last Wednesday, Sam had worried there would be that awkwardness between them again. Her fears were put to rest when she arrived after work Friday and Brooke seemed fine. She was rushing to get ready for the exhibition, but everything was normal. Then, Brooke got back Friday night, and everything was just…different again.

She tried to convince herself it was just tiredness, but the furrowed brows and faraway look on Brooke's face told her otherwise. It wasn't long before Brooke excused herself and went to bed. For what was probably the first time in a long time, Sam crashed on the couch and left early the next morning. She didn't want to read into things that weren't there, but her gut was telling her something was off, and her gut didn't like to be ignored.

The only thing she came up with was that maybe things had changed between Brooke and Dani. Maybe their non-date had become a date-date, and Brooke didn't know how to tell Sam after all her previous protestations. If that was it then Sam needed to figure out a way to let Brooke know it was okay. No matter how Sam felt or how badly her heart ached at the thought, she meant what she said to Brooke at lunch Wednesday. Above all else, she wanted Brooke to be happy. She would never be the one who stood in the way of that.

Sam had been lost in her thoughts and less than present with the excitable pancake monster across the table from her. Luckily, Finley was more than content to stuff his face with unlimited chocolate access, which Sam definitely should've monitored better, if the scene in front of her was anything to go by. She couldn't help but laugh at the confectionary-covered smile aimed her way as she suggested they call timeout on pancakes and make their way to the park.

They spent a fun few hours kicking around a ball Sam brought and played in the playground. Finley's laughter was exactly the right thing to soothe Sam's aching heart, and the playful afternoon worked wonders to calm her anxious brain.

As they made their way back to Brooke's house afterward, Sam spotted Brooke's car in the drive, and a mix of emotions overcame her. Happy, always, when she was going to see Brooke. But that was now tinged with apprehension. Would it be weird? She could pretend everything was normal, but that wasn't the right approach. Especially if Brooke was still treating her with kid gloves.

Sam opened the door and Finley ran in as Brooke came around the corner. She bent down to scoop him into her arms. "Hello, my little duckling." Brooke proceeded to kiss his face as Sam smiled, watching the display of affection fondly. "I'm not a duckling, silly Mama."

Finley giggled as Sam walked farther in, and Brooke glanced at her. For a moment, the world stopped turning as Sam braced herself. "What do you think, Sammy, is he a duckling?"

Sam could breathe again, and she laughed, joining in on the tickle party as Finley squirmed and squealed with delight. "Definitely the cutest duckling around."

They made their way into the kitchen, the sounds of Finley's laughter echoing along the hallway. Brooke had started an early dinner already and there were three places set at the table. Everything was going to be okay. It was just a regular Sunday afternoon. As they sat down to dinner, they talked about anything and everything. Except, Friday night.

"Sammy, where's your mama and daddy?"

Sam's fork full of food paused on the way to her mouth. Brooke's eyes were on her as she looked at Finley. Brooke spoke first. "Why do you ask that, kiddo?"

Finley shrugged and continued. "My daddy is in heaven. My nana says that Mama's daddy is there too. Mama's mom is in London which is kinda like hell. That's what Grandpa says." They both laughed at that. Jake's parents clearly had an interesting conversation around little ears. "Are your mama and daddy in heaven? Why I never got to meet them?"

Sam sighed. She wasn't going to get into the religion side of the conversation with the three-year-old. That was for another day. But she also wasn't going to lie to him. Brooke went to speak again, likely to save Sam from having to answer, but she held up a hand. "It's okay." She focused her attention on Finley. "I don't know where they are, buddy."

Finley's brows furrowed as he shot her a quizzical look. "They runned away?" Funny how the kid could hit the nail on the head with no information. "Yeah, something like that. I didn't have a family like you do, with your mama and grandparents and Aunt Maddie. You're a very lucky boy."

Finley looked at her, then smiled. "You're lucky too, Aunt Sammy. You have a family now. You got me and Mama." Sam's eyes welled, and she blinked back tears. She reached out and held his hand as he continued eating, oblivious to the emotions his innocent words created. She still felt the wounds he both opened and partially healed with his simple curiosity.

She looked up and caught Brooke staring at her, eyes filled with tears too. Brooke knew everything about Sam's past, of course. How she was abandoned by her mother after she was born and left with her father, who struggled with substance abuse, until she was taken into foster care at four. From there it had been a series of foster home after foster home, her anger and rage from the trauma that she remembered very little of now, combined with her misunderstood and mistreated neurodiversity, ensured that no one wanted to keep her for long.

Brooke reached out to grasp her free hand and squeezed hard as a tear slid down her cheek. Finley had one thing right. Sam was lucky. When Brooke walked into her life, she finally understood what it meant to mean something to someone. To matter. To have someone cry about your pain, care about your feelings, worry about you. It was everything.

She squeezed Brooke's hand in return and then hopped up from the table. "Who wants ice cream?" Finley's delighted agreement could be heard a mile away as Brooke huffed. "Pancakes with what I'm sure was way too much chocolate if that stained T-shirt is anything to go by, and now ice cream? You're putting him to bed tonight."

Sam laughed as she made her way to the freezer. She was more than okay with that.

❖

Brooke woke up the next morning and it was like something had landed on her head. If the pain was anything to go by, it was a very large boulder. Her eyes were heavy, she could barely breathe through her nose, and according to her throat, she had been swallowing pins and needles during the night. Finley bounced in and landed on her bed. She was in trouble.

No one warned you of the hell of being sick while being a single parent. She lifted her hand to her forehead and knew she was likely close to running a fever, but her demanding child needed breakfast. She went to sit up but thought better of it when the room spun around her. There was no way she was getting into work today, never mind making Finley breakfast or driving him to crèche.

She reached for her phone on the nightstand and rang the first number on her call list. "Sam, I need you." That would be enough, her hoarse and scratchy voice likely gave it away. Sure enough, no questions asked, she heard, "I'm on my way."

She handed Finley her phone with one of the kid's videos she had saved for times just like this and lay back down as he cuddled beside her. Barely ten minutes later, Sam came through the door and bounded up the stairs. She was definitely speeding. Brooke didn't even have the energy to reply as Sam called her name and came into the bedroom.

"Hey, kiddo." Finley jumped straight up and into Sam's arms. Brooke's eyes were heavier, but she opened them to focus on Sam's concerned expression. "Flu, I think. Dizzy. Can you drop Fin off before work?" She barely took in the reply before her eyes closed, assured that Fin would be safe now that Sam was here.

She woke what she assumed was a few hours later to something cool on her forehead. She reached her hand up and encountered a wet cloth. *How did that get there?* She opened her eyes and spotted Sam, sitting in a chair in the corner of the room, legs curled up and laptop propped in front of her.

"Sam?" Brooke's throat ached as her voice crackled.

Sam got up and came to her immediately. She picked up a glass of water from the nightstand and put the silicone straw to Brooke's mouth to take a sip. "How is the patient feeling?"

Brooke took stock. Her head was sore, she was a little hot, and her throat still ached, but the boulder was slightly lighter. "I'm okay. You stayed?"

Sam rolled her eyes. "What did you think I was gonna do, goof? I dropped Finley off and brought my laptop up here. I've been working while you slept."

Brooke smiled. She was still a little out of it. Sam passed her some of the cold and flu medicines which she took reluctantly. She hated taking medicine; it was like admitting defeat. Which was ridiculous. The birds that flew above her head when she tried to move had already defeated her.

"Thank you, Sammy Sam."

Sam laughed. "You look drunk."

Brooke huffed, but that's exactly what it was like. "I am not. The last time I was drunk, we had dirty hot sex. Right here."

Sam's eyes widened. Brooke found that she didn't even care, no embarrassment followed the statement. "I'm going to pretend you didn't say that because you have a fever. Also, you were definitely not drunk. Barely tipsy."

Sam was sitting on the bed, close but not touching. "It's not like we don't know it happened. It was good. You're an expert."

Sam put her head in her hands and groaned as Brooke laughed. Everything was funny right now. The laughter brought about a banging behind her eyes though, so she closed her lids again.

"So good," she whispered while sleep pulled her under as the medication took hold. Sam's hand lingered in hers and squeezed, as Brooke hoped she wouldn't let go.

When she woke later, her symptoms had improved dramatically. Sam was back in the chair, laptop on her lap being neglected as she gazed out the window. Brooke took a moment to look at her before Sam noticed she was awake. She was so beautiful. The way the light landed across her face made Sam's eyes glow and Brooke's heart catch. She didn't know if it was the medication or the fever, which she was sure had broken already, but suddenly she wanted nothing more than to pull Sam close and kiss her until the whole world fell away.

Sam turned her head back and caught Brooke's eye. She got up and moved toward her. "You okay there, B?"

Brooke nodded and found that her head was a lot less painful this time. "What time is it?" she whispered, her throat still ached when she spoke.

"Close to four. I asked Maddie to collect Fin, she's going to bring him to her parents for the night and drop him to crèche in the morning so you can rest."

Brooke nodded, too grateful for words. Sam always made things better. She was so lucky. "Thank you, Sammy. You fix everything. You're my favourite."

Sam smiled, her cheeks reddening. "Everything except your fever, clearly," she mumbled, grabbing the thermometer. She took Brooke's temperature and frowned. "Oh, the fever has broken, I think."

Brooke smiled, rolling her eyes. "I could've told you that, silly."

"I just thought, because you said…" The blush rose up Sam's cheeks as she trailed off.

Brooke frowned, then her eyes went wide. Oh no. "What did I say?"

Vague recollections whizzed through her brain. She couldn't remember what was real and what she had dreamt. *Please say it was a dream.*

"Nothing, just gibberish." Sam was lying. Brooke's head fell into her hands. The words *so good* swam around her brain.

"Oh God, Sam, I'm so sorry."

Sam laughed, shook her head and grabbed the cup on Brooke's nightstand. "Forget it, B. I'm gonna go make you some hot chocolate, and we'll throw on a movie. We can chill out for the evening, and you can get your strength back."

Brooke smiled and nodded. "That sounds like heaven. I love when you make hot chocolate."

Sam grinned, walked out the door, and threw out over her shoulder, "I know. I'm an expert."

Brooke giggled as she lay back to bury her face in the pillow.

CHAPTER TEN

The rhythmic noise of Brooke's breathing comforted Sam as her eyes fluttered open the next morning. They had fallen asleep on Brooke's bed watching a movie the previous night. Brooke was out cold during the first half, Sam finished the movie and took Brooke's temperature again, which luckily had stayed relatively low, before going to sleep.

Sam hated seeing Brooke sick, but she had to admit the fact that Brooke still called her the minute she needed someone, brought comfort to her. Whatever was going on between them, they were still, well, them. She placed a hand on Brooke's head. The fever was definitely gone now, but she was still a little clammy. Sam got up and grabbed water and more painkillers and placed them on Brooke's locker for when she woke before she hopped in for a quick shower.

The refreshing spray of water on her face was just what she needed to wake her up enough to start work. She had already decided to work from Brooke's house for the day. She wouldn't be much use in her office anyway when her thoughts would just be right here with Brooke. At least if she kept an eye on her, she had a chance of forcing her brain to cooperate with the latest project that had a far too tight deadline looming.

Not that having Brooke near helped in any regard with work yesterday. Aside from the worry, her mind was full of thoughts on how she was going to approach everything. There was no way they could continue to ignore what was, or wasn't, happening between them. Right? It wasn't smart. They had to address it. Figure it out. That was the mature thing to do.

It definitely wasn't healthy to pretend their bright idea of a one-night stand hadn't awoken far too many things inside her. Things she had no hope of getting past if her heart kept racing and her body kept tingling in all the right places every time she thought about it. Which she certainly couldn't do while naked in her best friend's en suite while the object of her attention slept a few feet away.

As she towelled off and mentally planned her morning, Brooke stirred in the bed. She threw her lounge pants and a T-shirt on and went to say good morning. A much brighter looking Brooke greeted her as she entered the room.

"You want breakfast?" Sam wasn't much for eating so early, but she was eager to get something substantial into Brooke since she barely ate a thing yesterday. As Brooke's eyes twinkled and she stifled a laugh, Sam threw her towel across the bed. "Listen, I may make a mess of pancakes but I'm sure I can manage some toast."

Brooke laughed and shook her head as she replied, "I'll grab a quick shower and make us an actual breakfast before you head to work." Sam was mid booting up her laptop, which she had abandoned on the chair last night, which to her dismay was being uncooperative.

"Well, I had planned to work here so I could take full advantage of your cooking for the day, but it looks like my laptop has other plans. I think I grabbed my old charger while rushing yesterday, which is somewhat temperamental."

"Feel free to use my laptop if it's any good to you. I've already called off work today. I feel a lot better, but I'm still tired and achy. I'm sure I'll also survive perfectly fine alone, although I'm iffy about how well you'd survive without my cooking." Sam laughed but couldn't deny it. She sucked when it came to anything culinary.

"That'd be great. I have everything I need for this project online so I can just log in from yours." Although Brooke did look much better, she'd rather stay near. Plus, it would save Brooke having to drive later if Sam grabbed Finley instead. As Brooke headed into the bathroom, Sam grabbed the laptop on her dresser and opened it up. She curled in the same chair she failed to work from yesterday, in a position she was sure would not be considered ergonomically best practice.

The screen came to life quickly as the laptop had been on standby. No matter how many times Sam told Brooke that her passwords sucked, she never listened. Brooke did most of her work in the office on her desktop, so her laptop was mainly used to store the numerous photos of Finley they took, and to watch movies from the comfort of bed.

The browser open in front of Sam made her brows furrow. Brooke often commented on how she had no clue how Sam found anything with the dozens of tabs Sam had open, so it was unusual for Brooke to have so many. But that wasn't the part that made Sam's stomach knot. It was that the photo she stared at right now looked like…her. One thing about having no family was that she had never really known what it was like to resemble someone. To look into someone else's face and see parts of your own reflected back. Until now.

Who was this person? And why, if the tabs were anything to go by, was Brooke apparently stalking her? Sam started to read the text next to the photo. It was a bio page on a website for an artist. Alexis Lynch. She was a local artist. Sam looked at the headings on the other tabs as her heart began to beat faster. Jumping to conclusions was never a good thing, but that's exactly what Sam's brain did.

Her eyes leapt to a tab that held a blog. She clicked over before she could think too hard about it and found herself reading an interview with the artist. The question currently highlighted on the screen in front of her was about the inspiration for her newest artwork. She talked about unknowns, about searching for where you belong, so many subtle things, until Sam read the one part that confirmed the suspicions that ran around her head.

I have family that I've never met. A sister. We didn't grow up together, but I know she's out there somewhere. I guess part of this has been a way to help me come to peace with the fact that I may always have questions about them and myself that I'll never get answered.

The words became blurry as Sam's eyes filled with tears and she bit her lip. Alexis. A sister.

Did she know their mother? Did she live with her? Was she her mother's second chance at getting it right? Sam's heart clenched. Being abandoned was hard enough to deal with. The constant feelings of never being good enough, never being wanted. What if Alexis had been good enough?

She sat frozen in space for what felt like forever. The distant sound of the water switched off. Brooke would be back soon. Brooke. How did Brooke know this? How long had she known? Then it hit Sam. Friday. The art gallery. That's why Brooke had been so strange. Had she known since then and said nothing?

Sam's thoughts began to spiral, and she started to get overwhelmed. So many things bombarded her as her throat began to ache from unshed tears. Tightness enveloped her chest as the laptop bounced on her shaking legs in front of her, but she was helpless to stop it. Her usual mantras weren't going to be enough this time. She didn't feel safe. She didn't feel secure. She needed to get it under control, but her whole world felt like it just fell from beneath her and she had no clue how to even begin to control that.

❖

Brooke was halfway through towel drying off, glad to feel far more like herself again, when it hit her, and her stomach lurched. Her laptop. She stood up quickly as she tried to remember if she had shut it off after spending so long poring over information about Alexis Sunday night. The sinking feeling in her gut pointed toward the answer being no.

The last thing she wanted right now was for Sam to learn from Google about the fact that she had a sister. As she walked out of her en suite and into her bedroom, the sight in front of her confirmed that she was out of luck with that wish.

"Sam." Brooke didn't even know what to say. To the outside world, Sam's face was blank. It gave nothing away. But Brooke knew better. She knew Sam. The glassy eyes, the shaking leg, the way she sat rigid in the chair, feet planted to the floor was more of a giveaway than any facial expression. She blinked when Brooke uttered her name again and her eyes rose, not quite meeting Brooke's, which was the best she was going to get right now.

"I'm sorry, Sam. I didn't mean for you to find out like this." Brooke walked toward the chair but as she saw Sam freeze, she thought better of it and sat across from her at the end of the bed. "Can you talk to me? What do you need?"

Sam wasn't being stubborn. She wasn't punishing Brooke with silence. Sam was likely spiralling and when that happened, often, no words were better than a tidal wave she couldn't control. Back in college, the first time Brooke ever saw Sam like this, it terrified her. She thought Sam was angry with her. She thought that was it, the end of their friendship even though she had no idea what had happened. All she knew was that Sam wouldn't speak to her and nothing she did helped.

Once Sam had calmed enough to talk then, she told Brooke she had bumped into a foster brother who opened up bad memories for her. Sam explained to her that when her thoughts got overwhelming like this, words were often hard to form. Not only that, she had a fear of speaking because when she was in an RSD episode, she couldn't always control the things she would say in the moment. After years of being punished and losing friends from lashing out, Sam learned to just stay silent until she soothed herself.

It was hard for Brooke to accept at the time because all she wanted to do was make Sam okay. Turns out, Brooke had been helping even if she didn't feel so at first. Sam explained that just listening to Brooke talk, knowing she wasn't expected to respond, helped Sam calm.

If Sam needed space or silence, then she knew to let Brooke know that. Otherwise, Brooke would talk until Sam was ready to. So that's what she did. Sam needed information. The more information she had, the quicker her brain would process the swirling thoughts inside it. So, Brooke explained, starting with Friday night.

"I was going to tell you when I got home Friday night, but you seemed so relaxed with Maddie and it was late and I just…I didn't know what to do. I didn't want to tell you something that could've been nothing. So, I figured I'd wait and talk to you Sunday."

"But you didn't." Brooke silently cheered at Sam's words. It wasn't much, and it wasn't positive, but it was words and that meant she was calmer.

"No, I didn't. I'm sorry for that, Sam. I spent the morning researching, trying to find out as much as I could so I had all the information to give you. I found the website, but it still didn't prove anything. I found an interview though and that seemed to indicate…"

"I know. I read it. So, there was no demanding client? Another lie?"

Brooke's heart sank at the bite in Sam's words, but she kept going. "No, there was no client. I wanted to find out more and talk to you on Sunday when Fin got to bed. But then Fin said that stuff at dinner about your parents running away and you looked so sad and I just…I didn't think it was the right time. I didn't know if you were ready to hear it. I figured maybe I should be completely sure before I opened a can of worms I couldn't close."

Sam was silent again, taking it all in. Finally, she spoke, and the crack in her voice made Brooke's decision to give her space no longer an option. "The can is open. I'm sure. I have a sister?" Brooke reached Sam's side as her sentence ended on a question that wasn't really a question. They both knew the truth. She wrapped her arms around Sam and waited a second for her to move if she needed to. As Sam melted against her, Brooke held her tighter as the tears fell. Both from Sam's eyes and her own.

After a while, Sam pulled back and dried her cheeks. "I really need to do some of this project." Brooke was going to object. Work wasn't as important as this. But by the look on Sam's face, she needed a distraction and time to process. Although Brooke was ready to dive right in and do whatever Sam needed, Sam had to deal with this in her way. For now.

Breakfast. She would help by making them food and giving Sam space to distract herself. As she reached the bedroom door, she glanced back to see Sam already engrossed in her latest design. No matter what Sam wanted to do, Brooke needed to be sure she understood she always had a family.

CHAPTER ELEVEN

The rest of the day passed quickly. They ate and talked about everything but the newest revelation in Sam's life. Brooke napped and watched crappy TV while Sam worked. Brooke said she was worried about Sam, but she still looked exhausted, and Sam insisted Brooke rest. Sam collected Finley from crèche after work and grabbed pizza for dinner. The drive allowed her time to think about what to do.

The car was always good for clearing her head. Initially, she had been angry with Brooke, but she understood. Brooke was trying to protect her. Sam processed better with information and Brooke understood that. But Sam just couldn't shake the feeling that everything was different. It was like she woke up and the world was a different colour. She just couldn't quite figure out if it was a better or worse shade.

When they got Finley to bed that evening, Brooke sat across from Sam and took her hand. "What do you want to do?" Sam had been anticipating this. Brooke gave her the space she needed today, but Sam had to figure this out. She sighed and shrugged. "I don't know. What if I'm wrong? What if she's just a random girl who looks like me and I'm over here having a crisis for nothing?"

Sam was clutching at straws, but Brooke replied anyway. "What if you're not? What if she's your sister, who knows about you and wants to know you? Is that something you want to find out?"

It was a loaded question. There were so many variables. Too many to account for. She was too jaded to believe that this was a fairy-tale ending to her story. *She finds her family and they all live happily ever after.* But could she live with this knowledge and never find out anything more? It was easy to ignore the urge to learn more when it was just a vague possibility. But this was a person. A real-life, tangible person that she could find out more about. Sam wasn't quite sure she could ignore that.

"What would I even do? Ring up this person and say, 'hey I think I might be your long-lost sister because you look like me and I read an interview where you said you had a sister'?"

Brooke stifled a laugh and Sam couldn't help but smile. She was always proud of her ability to make Brooke laugh in any situation. "You could email her? That might be easier than a phone call. It would give her time and not put her on the spot." Sam nodded as Brooke pulled out her phone and typed. Sam's phone pinged a moment later with a text from Brooke. An email address.

"So, when exactly did you become a stalker?" Brooke laughed again and shrugged at Sam's words. "Back in college when you avoided me for weeks? I had to gather information to woo you into being stuck with me forever." Sam shook her head and smiled at Brooke. "So that's how you knew what pizza to bring."

Sam stared at the email address in front of her, contemplating her next steps. She could ignore this. Pretend it never happened and go about her life. She had a family now, right? She had Brooke, Finley. She was happy.

She clicked on Compose New Mail because, despite her thoughts, she wouldn't rest until she found out more.

She typed out a quick email and handed it to Brooke. Short and sweet. Brooke read it aloud as Sam sat and fidgeted with the loose threads on the cushion she held in her lap.

"Hi, Alexis. I read an interview where you mentioned a sister—I think I may have information that might help you find her. Let me know if that's something you want, and I can send it to you. Thanks, Sam."

She figured this would be the best approach to take. If Alexis replied that she didn't want to find her, or didn't reply at all, then that was that. Sam didn't need to let her know who she was. Brooke nodded and handed the phone back and Sam pressed send before she changed her mind. Then they waited. Realistically, they had no clue how often Alexis checked her emails. Not everyone got them straight to their mobile like Sam. It could be days, weeks, hell even months if she even heard back at all.

That's what she kept telling herself until barely five minutes later the beep from her phone greeted her. Her screen flashed with one new email. Her heart thudded so loudly in her chest she swore Brooke would hear it. With shaky fingers, she unlocked her phone and clicked on the email. Brooke made no attempt to hide the fact that she was reading over her shoulder. Sam didn't care. She'd rather not have to relay the information, whatever it was.

"Sam, thanks so much for reaching out. My number is below. Please give me a call anytime, or an email. I'd love to hear any information you have. Thanks, Lexi."

Sam stared at the ten-digit number. Was it really that simple? Ten digits, one phone call away from learning more about her family than she had since as long as she recalled?

"Do you want to call?" Brooke's fingers on her arm snapped Sam out of her daze. There were a million excuses not to. It was late. She had barely had time to process. She should probably stick to email first, right? But the truth was she wouldn't sleep a wink until she did. She had gone this far, she wanted to see it through.

"I think I need to."

"Do you want me to wait in the other room?"

Sam gripped Brooke's hand and shook her head. "No, please, don't go."

Brooke settled back in the chair and held Sam's hand while her thumb stroked back and forth matching the deep breaths Sam took in preparation.

"I'm right here."

Sam took one last deep breath and focused on the warmth of Brooke's hand in hers. She could do this.

❖

Sam's hand shook in her grip as the phone rang. Brooke wished she could make it all better and do this for Sam. But this was something Sam needed to do for herself, so Brooke would do what she always did. She would be there for her every step of the way.

When Brooke met her, Sam was closed off, guarded. It took months to break through the walls she had erected around herself. It was a fluke that Brooke got through at all. So many others tried and failed, but Sam and Brooke clicked right from the start, despite Sam's attempts at keeping her at arm's length. Sam still had her moments over the years of shutting everyone out when things got hard, but Brooke waited her out, knowing she would talk when she was good and ready.

When Sam finally told her about her family, or lack of, Brooke's heart ached. How could someone as loving, kind, caring, and wonderful as Sam have been hurt so much? How was she a successful, amazing human being? Even back then, Brooke swore to herself that she would be all the family Sam needed, always.

Even throughout her relationship with Jacob, throughout the pregnancy with Finley, no matter what, Sam was her person. Jake understood; he loved Sam almost as much as she did. Now her son did, too. Sam was family, and it broke Brooke's heart that she had so much insecurity and doubt about herself because her parents couldn't be, well, parents.

Brooke shook out of her trip down memory lane as the dial tone stopped and a muffled voice answered.

She was only privy to Sam's side of the conversation clearly, but it was enough to get the gist of it. It was brief, Sam introduced herself, and they chatted for a few minutes. They made what sounded like arrangements to meet.

After the call clicked off, Brooke waited a minute to give Sam time to breathe, then asked, "So, how was it?"

Sam shrugged. "Weird. She said to call her Lexi, like her email sign-off. I guess she prefers the shortened version, like me. I didn't ask anything really because she suggested meeting after I explained I thought I might be her sister."

"Do you think you're ready for that?"

Sam took a breath. "I don't know. I don't think I'll ever know until I do it. She lives nearby, so we're going to meet at a café on Thursday after work. I figured I can ask the questions then. She seemed nice."

Sam sounded hopeful, but Brooke knew she must be a wreck on the inside. It was hard enough for her to let anyone in, let alone someone she didn't even know existed before yesterday.

The one person in the world who never had to face Sam's barriers wandered into the room rubbing his eyes. It was unusual for Finley to wake. He was usually out for the count after falling asleep. Clearly, his subconscious knew he was needed. He crawled into Sam's lap and snuggled into her.

"Hello, monkey." Sam grinned as she pulled Finley close. Brooke smiled at them.

If you looked at Sam as she laughed and cuddled Finley, most would never know anything was wrong. She was very good at concealing her feelings, which Brooke recognized early on as a survival technique. Brooke knew, though. There was a heaviness in Sam's eyes, and worry creased her forehead when a thought passed through her brain.

She let Sam bring Finley back to bed and get him settled again. While she was gone, Brooke grabbed extra blankets and headed to her room to get into her pyjamas. Finley's door creaked and she went out, took Sam's hand, and pulled her into her bedroom. "What are we doing?" Sam asked, confused.

Brooke smiled. "We're getting into comfy pj's, curling up under the blankets, and watching *Wynonna Earp*. How else am I gonna cheer you up?"

Brooke thought of a few other ways, but her brain was wise enough to keep those to herself. By the look that passed Sam's face, though, Brooke was pretty sure the thought crossed her mind too. Kickass demon-hunting heroines would have to do. Sam grinned and nodded her agreement.

As they changed and crawled under the covers, Brooke set up the laptop, and Sam lay close to her, and rested her head on Brooke's shoulder. They watched an episode and started another before tears fell from Sam's eyes onto Brooke's shoulder. They soaked through the thin material of her top. She put her arm around Sam and pulled her closer as Sam allowed the tears to fall unhindered.

"What if she hates me?"

Sam's whispered words made Brooke pull back. She lifted Sam's chin to look into her eyes.

"Impossible."

Sam shook her head to punctuate her point. "She might. She might want nothing to do with me."

Brooke wiped the tears from Sam's eyes and held her cheek. "She's the one who was looking for you, Sammy. That interview basically said so. She wants to know you. And once she does, she's never going to want to let you go."

"But they did. They knew me, and they let me go. They didn't want me."

Brooke couldn't think of the right words to say to make this okay. Sam was right, of course. But Sam's brain had a unique ability of turning things into the worst version of the truth.

"That wasn't about you, Sam. They didn't have the ability to provide what you needed. They couldn't be your parents. None of that was your fault. Do you understand me?" Sam nodded, but Brooke knew it wouldn't change the hurt it caused.

Sam looked into her eyes and gulped. "Why did nobody want me?"

Her voice broke on the last word, and Brooke's heart broke a little too. Sam had no idea how amazing she was, and Brooke had no words to prove it.

"I want you."

The words came out before Brooke stopped them. Suddenly, Sam leaned in, their lips crashed together, and she couldn't think of anything but making Sam's pain go away. Brooke gripped Sam tight against her and poured everything she couldn't say into the kiss.

Then her brain screeched to a halt. What was she doing? Sam was upset, vulnerable, not in her right state of mind. Here she was, about to take advantage of that.

"Wait, wait." Brooke put her hands on Sam's chest and moved back.

Sam scrambled from the bed, her face a mixture of hurt and embarrassment. "I'm sorry. Fuck, I shouldn't have...I should go."

Sam turned to walk away, and Brooke's heart started to beat frantically. "No, wait, Sam, it's not...I just can't. Not while you're so upset. This isn't right."

Sam walked backward until she reached the door and shook her head. "No, I get it. It's not right. I get it. I'm going to sleep in my room."

She was gone before Brooke had a chance to say anything more. Brooke knew she should get up and go fix this. Make it better. Comfort Sam. But she couldn't. She was terrified, paralyzed by the feelings surrounding her heart.

She couldn't give Sam what she wanted. She wasn't blind, she knew how Sam felt about her, and since the night they slept together, she couldn't stop seeing Sam in a whole new way. If she were honest with herself, she knew it began before their lips ever met. Dani's words in the carpark after their first and only date had opened the Pandora's box that led to that encounter.

Sam had always meant the world to her, but now there was an added layer of longing that Brooke couldn't switch off, no matter how hard she tried. But what if they tried giving this a shot and it didn't work out? Could they ever go back to what they were?

She had Finley to think about. He idolized Sam. And Sam... they were all she had. They were her family. How could Brooke risk that? Sam was going through so much right now, and she was supposed to be her safety net. But aside from all that, the truth was, Sam was the one person in Brooke's life who made her feel the most…her. Everyone else got pieces of Brooke, but she always held some back. Her mother got the successful, put-together pieces. Finley got the caring, motherly pieces. Even Maddie got the big sister, protector pieces.

But Sam? Sam was the only one Brooke never held anything back from. Sam was her sanctuary, her safe space, the only place in the world she felt free to be flawed and imperfect, but still be loved and accepted.

Brooke was dangling at the edge of a cliff, and whatever way she turned, there was a good chance she was about to fall. Images appeared in her head of the flashing blue and red lights outside her house. The garda at her door, the look on their faces as they told her that her husband was dead. The pain that had ripped through her body while her three-month-old baby cried as she wailed in pain.

She lay under the blanket and closed her eyes as she willed the images to stop. She knew one of the main reasons she wouldn't let herself go there was fear. She begged for the thoughts of losing Sam to go away. She couldn't take that risk. She sobbed into her pillow, as the one person who had the potential to dry her tears lay only feet away.

CHAPTER TWELVE

S am woke early and bleary-eyed the next morning. She had barely slept, her face still swollen from hours of crying. Her heart had shattered into a million pieces, and she couldn't begin to think about how to fix the mess she had made. Finley would be up soon, and she couldn't face him right now. She couldn't pretend to be okay.

She got up and dressed quickly and quietly and snuck out of the house. She ordered a taxi for down the road. It was childish, running away, but she couldn't deal with it all right now.

As soon as she got home, she sent a quick text to Brooke, letting her know she was home and safe. She held down the power button then, severing the inevitable communication. She ignored the work piling up on her laptop, grabbed her ebook, and got lost in her latest romance novel in bed. She sank into the cosy covers to hide from the world. Here, everything worked out. Everything made sense. The world wasn't a complete mess, and her carefully constructed life wasn't falling apart.

She woke suddenly, disoriented with the device still in her grip as someone pounded on her door. She pried her eyes open and dragged herself from the bed. For a moment she thought it might be Brooke, and her heart raced. Though from fear or longing, she didn't know. Except, Brooke would've just used her key.

She pulled open the door and Maddie stood there, face like thunder. "What the hell, Sam?"

Sam stood back as Maddie stormed in. She didn't know what to say. How much did Maddie know?

"Brooke rang me to thank me for helping out with Finley and she was crying. She won't tell me anything past you guys had a fight and you disappeared in the early hours of the morning. Which is a miracle for you as is, since you usually need to be dragged out of bed. It seemed like a big argument, if her face was anything to go by when I visited."

Sam sighed. Maddie knew nothing, other than Sam had somehow upset Brooke. That's all she needed to know to jump into protective sister mode. Something Sam marvelled at and admired despite her annoyance at the current disruption to her wallowing.

"Mads, don't take this the wrong way, but it's none of your business."

Sam wasn't in the mood for an interrogation. She wasn't in the mood for much of anything. Her thoughts were spiralling, but there was little to stop it at this point, beyond shutting it all out as she dove back between her covers to regulate her emotions in the best way she knew how.

"Sammy, what the hell is going on? You look like crap. Brooke looks like she didn't sleep a wink all night. What could possibly be so bad?"

Sam wasn't ready to get into anything, plus she didn't know what Brooke would want Maddie to know. So, she did the first thing she thought of…diversion.

"I have a sister. Lexi."

Maddie frowned. "You…what?"

They sat, and Sam explained what happened with the gallery and the phone call with Lexi and the fact that they planned to meet on Thursday. Which was now tomorrow. When she finally ran out of words, Maddie pulled her in and hugged her tightly.

"This still doesn't explain what happened with you and Brooke."

Damn, diversion didn't work. "Honestly, Maddie, it's nothing. I was being sensitive and got pissed that she kept it from me. It was foolish. We'll be fine, we always are."

Maddie looked like she wanted to push but thought better of it. "I know you'll be fine. You two love each other more than anyone I've ever known. There's no option but for you to be fine. You're family, Sam."

Sam's heart ached. What she said to Maddie might've been true, some part of her knew that they had to be fine, but she still had a hard time believing it.

Once Sam assured Maddie that she would be okay, along with promises to talk to Brooke soon, she got her out the door. She made tea and curled up once again with her book. Her mind kept wandering to the night before…the tears, the kiss. Why did she have to kiss Brooke again? Because she wanted to. At the moment, it just seemed so right.

But obviously not to Brooke.

Her cheeks flamed as embarrassment rose when she recalled Brooke pushing her off. She'd barely registered anything Brooke said, the shame and fear had clouded everything as she rushed to put distance between them. She'd made a mistake. One she couldn't make again.

How could she trust herself around Brooke right now while her emotions were so heightened? She needed some time. That was all. She would just take some space, get her head together, and figure out how to get back to being the supportive best friend.

Right now, she concentrated on the rest of the week. Work was going to be busy, but luckily, she had gotten a lot done to distract herself yesterday. She was both excited and terrified about the lunch with Lexi. Would they look as much alike in person as the photo? She never even asked Lexi her age.

Sam had yet to turn on her phone, so she grabbed it and powered it on. She had several missed calls—some from Maddie, most from Brooke. She also had text messages. She pulled up the latest one from Brooke asking her if they could talk.

She began to type out a response to politely decline but she stopped herself. She hated saying nothing though.

Time. Space. Maddie would tell Brooke she was okay. There was no need for her to ring right now.

She held her phone in her hand and willed herself to put it down. Even one day without speaking to Brooke was never easy. It was rare they ever went twenty-four hours. But she had to do it. Sacrifice the short term for the good of the long term. She needed to be sure she wouldn't blurt out something ridiculous or try to kiss her again or worse, tell her how she actually felt.

Which, she recognized, she still had to fully admit to herself.

❖

Brooke paced back and forth in her kitchen. Straight to voicemail, again. Damn it, Sam. Usually, by now she'd be at Sam's apartment, demanding she talk to her. Except for this time…she didn't know what she wanted her to say.

Her mind had been racing all night. She lost count of how many times she came close to walking into Sam's room and finishing what Sam started. Or begging her to talk to her. Or just being in her presence.

But she didn't. Something stopped her…and she knew exactly what that something was. Fear and shame.

How could she feel like this about Sam? Had it always been there? What did that mean about her and Jacob? No. She loved Jacob. They had been great together. Sure, she had always had a strong connection to Sam. A pull to her, a need to be around her. But that was normal for friends as close as they were. Kindred spirits, Jake always said.

He cared about Sam, too. He never had an issue with Sam being around. Even when they went on what most people would classify as "couple" holidays, he always invited Sam. He loved her. How could Brooke do this to him? What would people think? Maddie, his parents…

Jacob's family didn't think she would stay single forever, but how could she tell them she had fallen for Sam, of all people? They might think this wasn't a new development. *No. They wouldn't.* Jacob's family knew Brooke, they knew Sam. They would never think either of them would hurt Jake that way. Brooke dating anyone would be an adjustment, but she knew they'd never stop supporting her.

Aside from all of that, Sam was her family. She was way too important to risk everything they had built on something that might crash and burn. She thought about how she felt when Sam was around. The happiness, the safety, the complete and utter acceptance. Then she thought about how it would feel to lose that. She couldn't do that to herself, to Sam, or to Finley.

Sam needed a friend. She needed Brooke to be her best friend, that's all. Sam had a real chance with Lexi, a chance to answer a lot of the questions that took up so much space in her head. Brooke had to put her own confused feelings aside right now. She would go see Sam, talk to her, and tell her that she was there for her. They would be okay.

Brooke got into her car and drove to Sam's. She knocked, which was strange, but it didn't seem right to use her key. She got a flashback to standing on the other side of the door, waiting for Sam to open it in college, so much uncertainty about how the conversation would go. She knocked a few times before Sam's footsteps sounded and the door swung open.

"Maddie, I...oh." Sam stopped. "Sorry, I thought it was Maddie coming back. You didn't use your key."

"Can I come in?" Brooke noticed the slight tremor in her own voice. Sam frowned, then stepped back and gestured inside. Brooke walked in, feeling weirdly formal. This wasn't them.

Sam sat on the worn, light grey couch. The one Brooke helped her choose when they decorated this apartment all those years ago. Brooke hovered before eventually leaning by the edge. "Sam, I—"

Before she could finish, Sam cut in. "No, it's okay. You don't have to say it. I think...we need some space."

Brooke recoiled as if she had been punched in the gut. *Space? What was Sam talking about?*

"I have a lot on right now. With work and Lexi and…
everything. Emotions are all over the place. I think we should take
some time apart and re-evaluate."

Brooke's feet took over and she began to pace. "Sam, why are
you saying this? Why are you pushing me away?"

Tears threatened behind Brooke's lids as she attempted to
regain composure, but when she opened them again Sam's face
was stone cold. Not a hint of pain, sadness, nothing. Her walls
were well and truly in place.

"I just need to get my shit together, and I can't deal with all of
this now, Brooke. It's too much."

*What was too much? Brooke? Her feelings? God, this was so
messed up.*

"Sam, I'm your family. I'm your person. We deal with these
things together." She was bordering on begging now, and she
hated it, but she hadn't seen this side of Sam since the very start.
When Sam needed space throughout the years, she usually let
Brooke know it wasn't anything to do with her, it was never so…
dismissive.

Sam stood, walked to the kitchen, and started to pour herself
water. Her back faced Brooke as she spoke. "Not this time, Brooke.
I need to deal with this by myself. I need…I need you to leave.
Please, just go."

Brooke's tears fell unhindered, but Sam didn't even look
back. The pain in her chest intensified. This wasn't Sam. This
wasn't them. She knew it.

"Sam…"

Still, Sam didn't move. Her sigh carried across the small, yet
infinitely large space that separated them. "Brooke, for once can
you just do what I need and go."

That punch in the gut earlier was like a tickle compared to this
one. *For once?*

"What is that supposed to mean?"

Sam turned then, and Brooke wished she hadn't. The anger on
her face was like nothing Brooke had ever seen.

"I didn't want to say anything I'd regret, but you just won't listen. I do everything you need, Brooke. Everything. I am always there. I have been there for you for anything since…"

Sam trailed off and Brooke took over. "Since what? Since my husband died? I'm so sorry that was an inconvenience for you."

Brooke didn't know why she continued the argument. It was ridiculous, but anger was easier than the intense pain that was imminent.

"You know that's not what I meant. But this is the first time I'm asking you for what I need, Brooke. I'm telling you I need space; I need some time, and you aren't listening to me."

Brooke shook her head. "You're pushing me away. You're doing what you do. You're afraid, and you're putting your walls up. You can't do this. Whatever about me, you can't do this to Finley."

Brooke regretted the words immediately when Sam's face contorted in anger.

"I—how dare you? How could you think I would ever take any of this out on Finley? How could you—Just leave. Now."

She needed to stop but the words kept coming. "What exactly do you expect me to think? You think he won't notice if you're not around, Sam? What do I say, sorry she needs space? How do I explain that to a toddler?"

This wasn't fair. Brooke knew it, but she was clutching at straws. It wasn't fair to use Finley, and she hated herself for it.

"I will see Finley on Sunday for our date. I will call him during the week when he is with Maddie. I will never disappear on Finley, and I cannot believe you'd even think that."

"I know you wouldn't. But…you'd disappear from me? How exactly am I supposed to react to that?"

Sam slumped into the chair at the kitchen table. "I'm not disappearing. I'm just—Brooke, please. I've asked you to give me what I need. How else would you like me to say it?"

Brooke nodded. If she said anything more, she would make this worse and she knew it. She walked out, closed the door behind her, then leaned against it and let the tears fall. She had come here hoping to put her feelings aside and be the friend that Sam needed. It turned out, Sam didn't need a friend.

She didn't need Brooke at all.

Brooke took a moment and shook herself. She had to be honest, even if only with herself. Coming here wasn't just for Sam. She was afraid. Because if Sam didn't need her anymore…what did that mean? She sighed and stood straight, wiping the tears as she walked toward her car. Sam not needing her wasn't a bad thing. Brooke didn't need Sam.

But in that moment, despite the hurt, there was no denying how badly she wanted her.

CHAPTER THIRTEEN

The rest of the day passed in a blur. Sam tried to lose herself in work, doing her best to not think about Brooke. Which she failed at most minutes of the day, starting and deleting message after message. Her phone continuously drew her focus away from the website she was mid-building. But in the end, she sent none. She made the right choice. They would be okay eventually, but right now, she needed to protect herself. She couldn't face even more rejection.

Before Sam knew it, Thursday afternoon rolled around, and she was just about to meet Lexi for lunch. She arrived early to the café Lexi had chosen and took a seat in a booth by the window. Her heart raced, and her palms were sweaty. She ordered a tea and waited. And then waited some more. It was fifteen minutes past the time they had arranged and nothing so far.

Her heart started to sink. Why had she gotten her hopes up? She knew better than to rely on people. She checked her phone and found one new message.

Good luck today.

A simple sentence from the one person whose name had been running through her mind all week. She brought up Brooke's number and was just about to dial and wallow to her best friend about this when someone spoke.

"Sam?"

She looked up into honey brown eyes, so startlingly similar to her own that she momentarily just stared. The person who spoke had the exact same shade of ash blond hair as Sam, although longer than Sam's shoulder length. Her skin was a little tanner; Sam's was still a fair white, luckily not red from sunburn just yet. She had never seen anyone who looked so much like her, outside of the photo earlier in the week. At least, not that she remembered.

She blinked and shook her head. "Yes, I…Lexi. Hi."

Lexi smiled, sliding into the booth across from her. "Wow, this is strange," she laughed. At least she cut straight to the point.

Sam nodded. "Very strange."

They began to chat, Lexi apologized for being late. She warned Sam she was notoriously late, that getting caught up in her most recent artwork was a regular occurrence. Sam marvelled at how similar they were. Replace art with graphic design and it all lined up. Lexi was five years younger than Sam. They soon got around to the topic Sam was both desperate to know and terrified to hear about.

"Our mom…do you…did you…"

Lexi shook her head. "I don't know her. Sorry. I know you were probably hoping to find out more about her from me. I was one when she left me and my dad."

Sam didn't know how to feel. "I'm sorry. I guess she has a pattern. Your dad…did he stick around?"

Lexi nodded and a smile appeared on her face as she replied, "My dad is the best. He had his problems, but he got himself together and raised me by himself. He did his best."

Sam smiled, genuinely. She was happy for Lexi. She'd worried that she would be jealous, but only relief flooded her that Lexi hadn't gone through the system like she had.

"I'm happy to hear it. Looks like he did a great job."

Lexi beamed. Then her smile fell. "I'm sorry, Sam. I didn't think. You…your dad left too, right? I don't know much. I only found out about you recently when my dad told me."

"Don't apologize, I'm happy your dad was there for you. How did your dad know about me, though? Did she…did our mother talk about me?"

Lexi looked a little uncomfortable before she replied. "Apparently, they knew each other when she was with your dad. They were all friends, so he knew about you when you were born. They lost touch for a while until our mother fell off the wagon again, I guess. Neither of them were sober when they got together, before they had me."

Sam wasn't sure how to feel about that. Lexi's dad knew about her. That her mother had left her, that her father had been incompetent. Why did he even tell Lexi?

As if she knew what Sam was thinking, Lexi spoke again. "He feels really bad about it. About you. After he straightened out and got his life together to take care of me, he tried finding out what happened to you. He wanted us to know each other. He said an old friend let him know you were taken by social workers, but they wouldn't give him any information because he wasn't family. He was afraid to tell me, afraid I'd constantly wonder about you and blame him somehow. When he finally told me, all I wanted to do was find you."

Sam's heart lifted. Lexi wanted to find her.

Then she found herself doing something that shocked even her. She talked to Lexi. She told her about being taken from her dad and about being in foster care. Not all the nitty-gritty bits, but more than she'd ever divulged to a virtual stranger.

Lexi listened intently, no pity on her face. Just genuine concern and care. At one point during the conversation, she reached across the table and grasped Sam's hand. Sam didn't flinch or pull away. She tensed for a moment, then relaxed, allowing herself to enjoy the feeling of somebody comforting her.

By the time the hour was up, her heart was lighter than it had been all week.

"I'm sorry to leave, but I have to get back to get ready for a friend's party. I really wish we could continue."

Sam didn't doubt Lexi's sincerity. "Well, maybe soon? Dinner?"

Lexi readily agreed and they made concrete plans for that Saturday when she was off work. Sam left the café smiling, excited to spend more time with Lexi. Her sister. Suddenly, that word wasn't so scary.

She took out her phone to ring Brooke and tell her all about it but stopped herself right before dialling. No, she couldn't. Not yet. She wanted to tell her best friend about it, but that would lead to her calling to talk properly. And that would lead to—

Sam's brain jumped to the kiss. To Brooke's lips against hers, moving slowly. Hands on her body, caressing her as their tongues met and hearts raced. Sam shook her head. She couldn't even think about it without wanting to kiss Brooke. How could she be around her right now?

Until she stopped wanting to jump her every time she thought about her, she couldn't. Instead she shot off a quick text.

Thanks. Went well.

She needed to get this under control.

❖

Brooke sat at her desk as she anxiously stared at her phone every five minutes, willing it to ring. She never would've imagined that her best friend would be going through something monumental, possibly one of the most important days of her adult life, and Brooke couldn't be there for her.

She hoped the text message would let Sam know Brooke was thinking of her, without disobeying her request too badly. Just because she hadn't received a reply, it didn't mean anything, did it? Sam was busy. She was dealing with a lot. She was doing what she did to everyone. Everyone but Brooke. Withdrawing, pushing away. Sam would probably do the same with Lexi. Then she would have no one to turn to.

Brooke picked up her phone again, so close to dialling Sam's number, when her phone rang. Maddie.

"Hey, sis, how are you?"

Anxious, worried, annoyed, cranky. Brooke said none of those things, of course. "Fine, just finishing up for the day, you?"

Maddie sighed. "Not great. Carl is being an ass. Wanna come over to Mom and Dad's this evening? Bring kiddo to cheer me up?"

Carl and Maddie had been together since school. Maddie was barely a teenager when they first became friends, and he was her first crush. They rarely argued, so Brooke knew it was likely a bigger deal than Maddie made out. Brooke needed the distraction to stop her from contacting Sam again anyway.

"Sure. I'll just go collect Fin, and we'll be right over."

When she ended the call, there was a message from Sam. Her heart flipped. Then sank, as she read the contents. Three words. Since when did she get three-word replies? Feeling childish and fed up, her reply was even shorter. Not anticipating a response, she switched off her phone, got her stuff, and headed to her car.

After she picked Finley up and listened to him ask, once again, about Sam, she distracted him with the important job of picking out ice cream to bring to his grandparents. When they arrived, Finley was soon swept away by his grandpa to play with the train set that was more for Tom than it was for Finley.

Brooke made her way into the kitchen only to be shooed out by Lila. She loved Jake's mom and got on better with her than she ever had with her own. Brooke's mom had been living in London since her parents divorced when Brooke was a teenager, long before Brooke's dad died. She only visited a couple of times a year and had no interest in increasing that number. She sent presents, and they talked on the phone, but she was happy to be as absent a grandmother as she was a mother.

Lila took over that role the day Jake brought Brooke home to meet the family. She slotted right in and that had never changed. If anything, it had gotten stronger since Jake died.

"Go deal with my daughter outside. If she's not careful, that boy won't put up with her antics for much longer."

Brooke sighed. As nice as Lila was to her, she was just as hard on her own daughter. She made her way out back where Maddie was swinging on the set that had been there almost as long as she had. Brooke sat next to her and started swinging, knowing she didn't have to say a thing.

"I remember when we got this. I was about six. Jake pretended to be too cool for swing sets by that point, but secretly, he loved it. We would come out here most evenings under the pretence that he was just doing it for me. We would swing and talk about anything and everything. I never felt as close to him as I did out here."

Brooke could see the tears that welled in Maddie's eyes. Her heart was heavy. She lost her husband, and sometimes she forgot that other people dealt with the loss as much as she did. Maddie lost her brother, her only sibling, her partner in crime for most of her life. Jacob treasured Maddie more than anything. It was actually one of the things that drew Brooke to him in the first place. He was so proud of his baby sister and had no problem showing it.

Brooke reached out and took Maddie's hand. "He told me about that, actually. He said those were some of his favourite memories. He loved being out here with you. It was really special to him."

The tears started to fall from Maddie's eyes, and Brooke's weren't far behind.

"I miss him so much sometimes."

Brooke nodded. She didn't need to voice her agreement, though. They both knew it.

"I'm so glad I have you. That he brought you into our lives. Being here with you feels almost like being back there with Jake. Time has changed so much. I lost a brother, but I gained a sister."

Brooke squeezed Maddie's hand. No words encapsulated all she wanted to say in that moment, so she kept it short and sweet. "I love you, Mads, and Jake did too. Now…want to tell me what happened?"

Maddie sighed. "Carl wasn't being an ass. I was. I was stressed with exams and coming up to Jake's anniversary, and I took it out on him. I need to apologize."

Brooke froze. She didn't move or speak. Maddie looked at her, concerned. "Brooke? Are you okay?"

"Jake's anniversary. It's next week."

Maddie frowned and nodded. "Yeah, I just said that."

Brooke's heart beat like it was about to implode. Maddie looked confused, then her eyes widened. "You forgot."

Brooke closed her eyes. Shame, guilt and anger filled her body. Jacob would be gone three years, and she forgot. An arm went around her shoulder and she pushed it away. "Don't. Don't comfort me. How could I forget? What kind of person am I?"

Maddie held her tighter. "Brooke. You have a lot on. Life gets in the way sometimes. The last thing Jacob would have wanted is for you to be counting down the days to his anniversary. You're raising his son, you're working, you're moving on. That's not a bad thing."

Maddie was trying to help, but all she focused on was the last part. She was moving on. She went on dates. She was…whatever she was doing with Sam. She was forgetting him.

Sam came into her mind then, and Brooke's anger intensified. She should be able to ring her right now and talk about this, but she couldn't because Sam was too busy being angry at the world. Brooke was so worried about Sam that she forgot about this. Not anymore.

As if Maddie read her thoughts, she hesitantly asked, "How are things with Sam?"

Brooke shook her head. "I wouldn't know. She doesn't want a friend right now."

Maddie squeezed her shoulders. "Even if that were true, you're not just her friend, Brooke." Brooke's heart started to race until Maddie continued, "You're her family."

The words started another flow of tears, and this time, it was Maddie who held Brooke's hand for comfort.

"You know Jacob would want you to be happy. My brother was a bonehead, but he loved you more than anything in the world. He would want you to feel that love again. No matter who it was with."

Maddie left those words hanging between them as Finley ran outside, a bundle of energy. Brooke quickly wiped her tears. "Aunt Maddie!" He ran straight into her arms, and they started to swing back and forth.

Brooke was relieved the conversation was over; it was getting too close to a place she wasn't ready to go. She watched her son, who looked so much like his father, and smiled. She would always have a reminder of Jacob in Finley.

"Can I call Sam now, Mama?"

Brooke rolled her eyes. She'd always have a reminder of Sam, too, it seemed.

CHAPTER FOURTEEN

One week. Seven days. That's how long it had been since she'd seen Brooke. Probably the longest in at least five years. Sam picked Finley up from Maddie on Sunday for their date. She was both relieved and disappointed when Maddie texted to say Finley was with her. Sam assumed Brooke went out with Dani on Saturday night. She ignored the stab in her chest at that thought.

It was Wednesday, the second time they would miss their lunch date. Sam was all too aware of that fact. Lexi invited her to her latest art exhibition that night. She was actually looking forward to it.

But something was missing, and Sam knew it was her best friend. She missed the ease when they talked. She missed how Brooke knew what Sam was feeling even before Sam did. She missed knowing that there was one person in the world she could talk to about anything with no judgment. She missed Brooke with an intensity that proved to her, no amount of waiting around for these feelings to subside was going to work. The longer she avoided this, the harder it was going to be.

Sam picked up her phone. Brooke hadn't reached out past those messages last week, but Sam had asked her not to. It was the longest they had gone without talking since she remembered. Sam had to make the first move.

She rang Brooke's number, willing her to pick up. It rang and rang and eventually went to voicemail. Brooke was avoiding her. She always had her phone with her at work. Sam sighed. She had asked for this, so she couldn't really complain.

She closed her eyes and leaned back, then her heart sank. She checked the calendar, then sank even further into her seat. It was Jacob's anniversary. What kind of friend was she? How could Brooke ever forgive this? Not only had Sam been cold to her, pushing her away and not answering her last message, but she also forgot her husband's anniversary. Didn't even message, never mind show up and be there for her.

The past two years on Jake's anniversary, Sam had been there. They had celebrated his life together, doing things he loved to do and telling Finley the best stories about his dad. They ate his favourite foods and ice cream and then finished off the evening with Maddie, watching the stars on the beach like they used to when they were in college.

She ached to be there now, doing all those things. For Brooke mostly, but also for herself. She had loved Jake like a brother. She couldn't believe he was gone three years already. She remembered the night he died like it was yesterday. A drunk driver ran a red light and Jake didn't stand a chance.

She remembered the incoherent voicemail she had received from Brooke. The terror as she drove to the hospital, no idea what she was going to be met with. Sam was lucky she understood the hospital name in Brooke's message and just went straight there. The rest was a blur. She was already numb when she heard he was dead on impact.

After that, she had gone straight into taking care of Brooke mode. Her ability to excel in a crisis was a part of her neurodivergence she was thankful for then. She helped arrange the funeral, helped take care of Finley who was just a baby, and made sure that Brooke ate. She didn't leave her side for weeks. She worked from Brooke's house, pretty much moved in there for months. She had never been so grateful to be self-employed as she was then. Working from home, well, Brooke's house, helped with easing her worry about Brooke and taking care of Finley. Especially on the days where Brooke could barely make it out of bed.

She was there through it all. Every step of the way, as any friend would be. But where was she now? Nowhere to be seen. Brooke deserved so much better than this. So did Finley.

She packed up her work stuff and started to make a plan in her head. She needed to make this up to them, and she needed to do it now.

She locked up the store and grabbed the bus home. She would need her car to go get supplies. When she got there, she picked up her phone to try Brooke again before she left. One voicemail. How had she missed the call? As she listened to the message her heart started to race, and she sank into a chair. She heard Brooke's sobs, then the name of the hospital and—

Finley.

No. Not again.

She grabbed her car keys and bag and fled from the apartment. She needed to stay calm enough to drive to the hospital and see what had happened. She couldn't fall apart. Brooke needed her; Finley needed her.

Her family needed her.

She pulled into a parking spot at the hospital fifteen minutes later. The automatic doors of the hospital loomed ahead. Sam briefly had a momentary déjà vu as she recalled walking through these same doors three years before. After some enquiries, she headed in the direction of the accident and emergency department. Brooke paced the corridor up ahead, and Sam ran straight to her.

"Brooke, what's going on? Where's Fin?"

Tears leaked from Sam's eyes before she stopped them. Without speaking, Brooke pulled her into a hug and crushed Sam tightly against her.

Sam held her tight, but her heart was in her throat. What did this mean?

"Please, B. Finley?"

Brooke pulled back. "He's okay. Well, he will be." Sam released a sigh of relief and she could breathe freely for the first time since she listened to the message. She sat in a chair in the corridor and Brooke sat next to her.

"He fell off a slide in crèche and broke his arm just above his elbow. I'm sorry for the dramatic voicemail. I hadn't even gotten here yet. I just rang you as soon as I got off the phone from the crèche, and I didn't know how bad it was."

Sam held Brooke's hand in hers. "Don't apologize. Where is he? He must be in pain."

Brooke nodded. "He's in surgery. They just took him down before you got here. They need to operate on his arm, but they said he'll be fine. He was in pain when I got here, but he was telling me all about it."

Surgery sounded so scary to Sam. He was so little. But she didn't want to worry Brooke any more than she already was. "He'll be fine, he's a superhero."

Brooke smiled at her, her face still red from the tears that had clearly only recently abated. "He'll be happy you're here when he wakes. If you can stay."

She grasped Brooke's hand tightly. "Of course I'm staying."

Brooke nodded, and they sat in silence for a while, hand in hand, eyes glued to the clock. After what seemed like an eternity, the surgeon came out to let them know that it had gone well, and Finley was in recovery. They could see him soon.

They both visibly relaxed in relief and smiled at each other.

"I'm so sorry, B." Sam's voice was barely a whisper, but Brooke heard her. It wasn't the time or place to get into any of this, but she couldn't help it. She had to say it. The guilt was gnawing at her gut, and it needed to get out.

"Me too, Sammy."

They stared at each other for a few minutes, and Sam went to speak, when the doors opened and in walked Dani.

"Brooke, how is he?"

Sam pulled her hand out of Brooke's, unsure of what to do or say, just knowing she needed to move. Brooke reached toward her, but she backed away quickly. Dani looked at her, frowning.

"I…I'm going to go get us food and coffee. Food will make everything better. Be right back."

She turned and walked away before they had a chance to reply. Of course, Brooke had messaged Dani. It's not like Sam had been the most reliable friend lately. Just because Sam was about to tell Brooke the truth of her feelings didn't mean that Brooke wanted to hear it.

She was thankful for Dani's timing. If anything, it had saved Sam from making a fool out of herself again.

❖

Brooke tried to concentrate on what Dani said to her, but her eyes were stuck on where Sam had left. She ached to go after her, but everything was still so raw.

"Brooke?"

She finally snapped out of it and looked at Dani, who was looking at her with concern etched all over her face. "I'm sorry, what were you saying?"

Dani sat in the chair Sam had occupied moments ago and took Brooke's hand. "How's Finley?"

"He's okay. Out of surgery and in recovery. Thank you for coming, you didn't have to."

Brooke only remembered her plans to meet Dani for lunch when her phone rang on the way to the hospital. She had blubbered the gist of what happened to Dani on the call, but she never expected her to show up here.

Brooke paced, eyes still veering back to where Sam had disappeared. "I'm a bit of a mess right now. Obviously because of Finley, plus—"

"Plus, you love Sam. You need to tell her." Dani cut in before she finished.

This wasn't the time or place for this conversation, but Brooke didn't have the capacity to deny it either.

Dani smiled, squeezing her hand. "Brooke. She loves you too, don't you see? It's obvious."

Brooke frowned again. "It is?"

Dani nodded. "To everyone but you and Sam, apparently. It's all over her face, and yours too."

Brooke nodded. Of course she knew. That wasn't the issue. She didn't doubt Sam had feelings for her.

"I'm sorry. You really are an amazing person and I haven't been the most present of friends. You came all this way from one phone call. I appreciate it, more than you know. But I really need to go find her."

Dani stood and pulled Brooke into a hug. "Don't apologize. Don't be a stranger. If you need a friend, just call. But right now, you and Sam need a little time to figure this out together."

Sam appeared just as Brooke pulled back. Dani placed a kiss on her cheek, waved to Sam, and walked away.

Sam approached and sat down, handing Brooke a prepackaged sandwich and a cup of coffee. "Dani had to leave already?"

Brooke nodded, but didn't offer any more information. Telling Sam why Dani left would lead to a conversation they weren't in the right place to have. But it was one she was getting more and more sure they needed to have. Her stomach flipped at the thought, but for once, she was sure it held less fear and more anticipation.

The doctor came out just as they finished their sandwiches and led them into a room where Finley was still sleeping. He looked so tiny in the big hospital bed. Sam went straight up to take his hand and stroke his hair. Brooke stood back, the tears that had only recently stopped making tracks down her cheeks again.

Three years ago today, she had stood in this exact hospital. The outcome had been very different then, and she had been left a widow and a single mother. Here she was, three years on, with her son, whose face resembled his father's so much. She should be happy that it was only a broken arm. It would heal. But she couldn't help but think of how different it might have been.

Sam turned and reached out to Brooke. She walked toward her, pulling her into her arms as Brooke sobbed. She kissed her forehead and held her tight, allowing her to cry. Suddenly, they were greeted with the sweetest sound.

"Mama? Sammy…"

They both turned and rushed to Finley's side as his beautiful brown eyes flickered open.

Brooke couldn't speak for fear of crying again, but Sam stepped in. "Hey, kiddo. You gave us a scare doing your superhero stunts."

Finley's face split into a sleepy smile. "Sammy, you here." He croaked.

"Of course I'm here, monkey. There's nowhere else I'd be."

The familiar warmth of Sam's hand landed in Brooke's as her other clutched Finley's tight. Brooke was so thankful that this woman had entered her life. She had been there for her through everything, especially over the last three years.

As Finley woke more completely, they got the full re-enactment of what happened. Sam excused herself after a couple of hours to go get them dinner. Brooke had told her to go home because it had been a long day, but Sam wouldn't think of it.

"I saw Daddy."

Brooke looked up from the magazine she was reading as Finley woke from another sleep. "You did, baby?"

Finley nodded. "Yes, in my dreams. We played games."

Brooke's throat clogged. She swallowed it down and pasted a smile on her face. Her son had seen her cry far too often lately, as much as she tried to hide it.

"That's great, Fin. Did you have fun?"

Finley nodded again, his smile a mirror image of his father's. "Yes. He said hi to you and to Sammy."

Brooke smiled and kissed her son's head. He often had dreams of his dad. She loved that he thought of him even when he was in pain and hurt. They made sure he always felt like he knew Jacob.

Sam walked in the door then, and Brooke laughed. It was perfect. In one hand was a takeout bag from Jake's favourite Chinese takeaway. Her other hand clutched a pint of his favourite cookie dough ice cream. Sam grinned at Brooke's laugh, clearly relieved that it was received well.

"Daddy's ice cream!" Finley perked up immensely at that.

They sat and ate the food and ice cream and talked about Jacob. They told Finley more stories of Jake's antics in college and how much he loved playing with Fin when he was born. A short while later, Maddie, Tom, and Lila showed up. Brooke had told them not to come earlier since only two people were allowed in the room before visiting hours.

They fussed over Finley, and he was delighted with all the attention. Before it got too late, Sam asked Tom and Lila to sit with Finley, and asked Brooke and Maddie to follow her. She led them out to the carpark and grabbed a blanket from her car. The sun had set, and the stars twinkled above them.

They walked to the park across from the hospital, and Sam laid out the blanket so the three of them could lie down and stare up.

"It's not quite the beach, but it's the best we've got."

Brooke lay staring at the stars above, an action that always brought Jacob to mind for her, and she remembered Finley's dream. Jake was always going to be a big part of their lives, but she knew Sam and Maddie had both been right before. He would want Brooke to be happy—he would want that for all of them.

She linked her fingers with Sam's and smiled. "It's perfect."

CHAPTER FIFTEEN

Finley was discharged the following day with a cast, painkillers, and an appointment to return for a checkup in four weeks. Sam followed Brooke's car to her house and helped get him settled on the couch with his favourite cartoon, blanket, and snacks.

Once he was comfortable, Sam hovered a moment, suddenly unsure what to do. Things had been all about Fin in the hospital, and up until this point, she hadn't really taken the time to consider that things might be awkward now.

"Want to watch a movie with us and stay? If you can. Fin would love it."

Brooke appeared a little nervous as she asked, but Sam readily agreed. She was ready for things to go back to normal between them, and this was the perfect opportunity. Plus, she'd just worry about Finley if she wasn't here anyway.

They threw on the movie as her phone started to ring. She excused herself and walked into the kitchen to answer.

"Hey, I think I'm at your place but there's no answer. Is it the red door?"

Lexi. Oh no. Sam had completely blanked on the exhibition.

"Lexi, I'm so sorry. I completely forgot." Sam put her head in her hand. She was the worst. Here they were, just getting to know each other and she left Lexi standing outside her apartment alone.

"You forgot? Where are you? Do you want to meet me there?"

She noticed the confusion in Lexi's voice, and she didn't blame her. The familiar worry crept in. "I can't. I'm sorry. Finley broke his arm and he had to have surgery, and everything just slipped my mind."

Sam started to pace the kitchen as guilt gnawed at her insides.

"Oh no, is he in hospital?" Lexi sounded genuinely concerned, and Sam sank deeper into shame.

"He was. He's home now. We're just watching a movie."

She braced herself. This was it, right? The time her forgetfulness ruined a relationship before it even had a chance.

"No wonder it slipped your mind. I hope he's okay. What movie are you watching?"

Sam blew out a breath as Lexi's voice stayed light. No hint of annoyance or frustration. "*Finding Nemo*. Listen, Lexi, I really am sorry. I would come, but I just—"

"No, no, seriously, there will be plenty of these. You'll come to the next one. Give Finley my best, and don't stress."

Brooke appeared in the doorway. How much had she heard? Sam worried Brooke would demand she go, and it would make things awkward again.

Sam signed off and hung up. She felt bad, but Lexi helped lessen her guilt which she was grateful for.

"Everything okay?" Brooke stood with worry lines creasing her forehead. "If you need to go it's okay."

Sam shook her head. "No, I'm where I need to be. Just going to grab a drink."

Brooke smiled and went back to Finley. Sam shot off a quick text to Lexi to apologize again and wished her luck on the exhibition. Then she switched her phone off and grabbed a drink, heading back in to watch the movie.

The next morning, Sam had to go into work to meet with a client but promised Finley she'd come back after. She swung by her apartment to pack a bag for the weekend once she finished up. She wanted to help out as much as Brooke needed.

Sam got back to the house with pizza boxes in hand and was met with a gleeful hello from Finley. As if she hadn't just seen him that morning. Brooke was getting off the phone when Sam entered the room. A smile that made Brooke's beautiful blue eyes sparkle appeared.

"You look almost as happy to see me as Finley. Or possibly the food. It's the food, isn't it?"

Sam grinned as Brooke gave her signature eye roll. Sam wasn't surprised at how much she had missed it.

They ate and chatted. Sam told Brooke all about her initial lunch with Lexi, and their previous dinner. She also explained about last night, which Brooke grumbled about. Brooke told Sam she should have gone with Lexi, but by her expression, Brooke was thankful she hadn't.

"Ask her to come to lunch Sunday. You can introduce her to the family."

Sam's heart warmed at that statement, knowing Brooke meant her and Finley.

"Come to lunch, like here?"

Brooke nodded. "Yeah. Don't worry, I'll prepare lunch. You are not poisoning your sister before you get a chance to know her properly."

Sam pretended to frown, but a laugh quickly escaped. Brooke had a point. She sent a quick text to Lexi with the request and got a positive reply asking for the address within a few minutes. She was suddenly very excited for Sunday.

"If you want to go out, like with Dani or anything, I can stay with Fin tonight or tomorrow night." Sam knew she should at least offer.

Brooke shook her head and kept her eyes averted. "No, I'm good. I told you, Dani and I are just friends. I think I'm putting a halt on the dating thing for now."

Sam frowned. What? So many questions ran through her head. "What happened?"

Brooke avoided her eyes as she mumbled, "It just isn't the right time. I'm not ready. I need to focus on Fin."

Sam knew bullshit when she heard it, especially from her best friend's mouth. Brooke had been ready for the last year.

"Brooke. Finley has been and always will be your main focus, but you need to do this for you. Don't push Dani, or anyone, away just because of what happened. He fell at crèche, and nothing you could have done would have prevented that."

As Sam tried to convince the best friend she fantasized about kissing, much too often lately, to date another woman, she marvelled at the absurdity of it all. But Brooke needed to let herself be happy. Sam didn't want her giving up on that chance. Especially if they were going to broach the conversation that was brewing beneath the surface.

Brooke shook her head. "You don't understand." She got up and cleared the table.

"Clearly, I don't. Dani seemed to make you happy, and you keep insisting you're just good as friends. You're pushing her away." Sam frowned. She wondered if Brooke realized at the same time she did what she was really saying. She wasn't speaking about Dani at all.

"Well, you'd know all about that." Brooke shot the words out and then stopped.

Sam froze. "Low blow, B."

"I'm sorry, Sammy, that was a crap thing to say." Brooke dropped her head and walked over to sit next to Sam. She reached out to rub her thumb along Sam's hand and locked their pinkie fingers together.

"Well, it was true. But look where that got me. I was miserable not talking to you. I didn't push Lexi away, and it may lead to something wonderful. You need to allow yourself to feel again, Brooke."

Brooke looked up and stared into her eyes. She licked her lips, and Sam's heart raced. She needed to get herself under control, quickly.

Finley called for Brooke from his throne in the living room and they both snapped back to reality. Saved by the toddler, again. This was becoming a habit; Sam needed to buy him more chocolate.

Brooke squeezed her hand and got up to walk away.

"We'll continue this later. You're not off the hook." Sam smiled at the fact that she knew Brooke was rolling her eyes at Sam's words without even seeing her.

❖

"I forgot."

It was later that evening; Finley had gone to bed, and they were on the couch. The television played in the background, but Brooke had no idea what was on. Her head was far too full from their earlier conversation. Sam turned down the volume after Brooke spoke.

"You forgot what?"

Brooke turned toward Sam, mirroring her actions as she fidgeted with the blanket. "I forgot about Jake's anniversary."

Just those words created a host of shameful feelings in Brooke. It had spun around her head all evening. Although she still couldn't voice to Sam the real reason she and Dani wouldn't work out, she could tell her this.

Sam grasped her hand. "So, it slipped your mind. Brooke, that's not the end of the world. Is that why you're deciding you're not dating anymore?"

Brooke didn't want to lie to Sam. Instead, she artfully dodged the question.

"How could I forget him, Sammy? It's only been three years, and already I forgot his anniversary. If for nothing else, I need to keep his memory alive for Finley. A few dates and he's gone from my mind already? No."

Brooke shook her head and gripped Sam's hand.

"You forgot his anniversary. You didn't forget him. Are you telling me you didn't think about him at all? I know that's not true.

You tell Finley stories about him all the time. You have pictures, scrapbooks, videos. You always make sure Finley remembers him, so don't you dare get down on yourself about that. Finley needs to see his mom happy, more than anything else. He needs to know it's okay to be happy even without his dad here. You are that example for him."

Brooke blinked. She hadn't considered it that way. She knew she was being irrational about the anniversary, but it seemed like so much more than that. Everything was changing, and it was too quick. Her life was comfortable with Finley and Sam. Before that night, everything was good. Right? Content, at least. Content was nice. It was better than the swirling ball of confusion that had been in her gut more often than not the past few weeks.

"You're right. But I still think it's the right decision with dating. I need to take everything at a pace I'm comfortable with and everything right now is just too much. I'm not giving up forever, I promise. I'm just not ready right now."

Sam bit her lip but didn't say anything further. She squeezed Brooke's hand and turned the volume back up. They watched in silence for the rest of the night, fingers still entwined.

Brooke woke up with a weight on top of her. She blinked open her eyes and took a minute to figure out what was going on. She was still on the couch, with Sam snuggling against her, half on top of her body which must have stretched out along the couch during the night. Brooke's arm was draped around Sam, resting against the small of her back.

The room was dark, so it wasn't quite morning yet. She had an ache in her neck from the angle, and her back screamed to be adjusted, but there was no way she was about to move. She pulled Sam closer and let her lids fall shut. This earned her a contented sigh. Sam burrowed against her, moving to nestle her head in the crook of Brooke's neck. Brooke's heart beat faster but she ignored it. Right now, she wasn't questioning, she wasn't overthinking. She was just happy to hold Sam, regardless of what that might mean.

She must have fallen back to sleep because the next thing she knew, she awoke to the smell of something burning. Her eyes flew open. She was alone on the couch, and she heard muttered cursing coming from the kitchen. Finley ran in, noticed her awake, and announced, "Sam's burning everything again."

Brooke smiled sleepily and got up. Of course she was. She walked toward the kitchen, grabbing the kiddo for a hug on the way.

"Don't even say it," Sam muttered as Brooke walked in.

The place was a mess. There were the remnants of pancake batter strewn around the countertop. Flour covered the floor and most of her son's clothes, which she only now noticed. Many more eggshells than what should be needed for pancake mix lay next to a bowl.

Then there was the frying pan which a frazzled looking Sam held in her hands as she scraped what Brooke could only assume was supposed to be a pancake into the bin.

Finley tugged at Brooke's pants and pointed up. Brooke looked at her ceiling where an impressive outline of grease marked the white paint. She looked back at Sam, one eyebrow raised.

"Just don't say it."

Brooke laughed and set Sam and Finley to the task of cleaning up while she went about making what she now knew would be the third bowl of pancake batter of the morning. She set the pancakes in front of a glaring Sam and a grinning Finley and smiled.

The world was right again.

CHAPTER SIXTEEN

"Sam, stop pacing."

Brooke's hands landed on her shoulders to stop her in her tracks. Her heart was beating frantically. It was 12:50 p.m. Lexi was due in ten minutes and Sam was panicked. Which made no sense. They had gotten on so well when they met and every time they had talked since. Sam knew they had a lot in common and she knew Lexi was nice. So why was she freaking out?

"I don't know what's wrong."

Sam looked at Brooke helplessly as her mind raced.

"You're nervous. That's okay. Your worlds are colliding right now. Your sister is meeting your family and that's a lot. That makes things more real, right? It's okay."

Sam nodded. That made sense. Brooke always made her racing thoughts seem rational.

She began to breathe a bit easier as Finley walked in. He wore a pressed white shirt and pink unicorn tie, his choice. Sam smiled.

"Well, don't you look dashing, young man."

Finley grinned. He insisted on wearing his *special occasion clothes* to meet Sam's sister. He was on a mission to impress.

The doorbell chimed and all three heads swivelled toward it. Sam took a second to breathe in and out, then walked toward the door. Brooke held a bouncing Finley back and warned him to give them a minute. She opened the door and was once again struck by the similarities between them. She was at ease instantly, as she looked into the face so like her own.

She invited Lexi in and smiled at the chocolates she held out. Fin would be happy with the offering.

"Whoa."

The whispered word came from behind her. Finley crept up and snuck an arm around Sam's leg as he stared and whispered, a little too loudly, "She looks just like you, Aunt Sammy."

Lexi immediately bent down to his level, smiling wide.

"Why hello there. I love your tie. What's your name?"

Finley nestled his head against Sam's leg. Sam smiled. Finley rarely actually resembled the three-year-old that he was. He spent time around adults so much that he was used to having conversations well above his level. Sam often forgot his age, until times like this. Finally, he plucked up the courage to speak.

"I'm Finley Jacob Fields." He stuck out his hand to Lexi.

Sam laughed at his formality as Lexi shook his hand and grinned.

"Well hello, Finley Jacob Fields, I'm Alexis Kathleen Lynch. But you can call me Lexi."

Finley smiled as Brooke stepped forward. "Hey, Lexi, I'm Brooke, this gentleman's mom. Although I feel like I have two kids at times, with this one."

She pointed toward Sam who looked indignant. "Don't believe a word she says." Sam huffed, walking toward the kitchen. The table was set with more food than the four of them could possibly consume. Brooke went all out.

"Wow, this looks amazing, Sam." Lexi stared in awe. Sam held her hands up. "Honestly, I had nothing to do with it. Brooke doesn't let me cook. She's a control freak." Brooke swatted her with the towel she held after washing her hands.

"Sorry. I like my kitchen not on fire." Lexi's head moved back and forth between them, a look of amusement on her face. They settled down to eat and chatted easily. Finley became much more animated as he got used to Lexi being there.

"Sammy said that you are her sister. I didn't know Sammy had a sister. She said neither did she. How you have a sister and not know?"

Lexi was caught off guard but recovered quickly. "Well, that's a good question. Sam and I didn't grow up together like most sisters. I lived with my dad."

Finley nodded. "Not your mama?"

Lexi shook her head. "No, not my mama. But my dad got married again later and so I have a stepmom."

Finley frowned at the unfamiliar word. "What's a stepmom?"

Sam watched the interaction, debating whether to hop in to save Lexi, but she seemed to have it under control. "Well, it means my daddy loved somebody else after my mama was gone. She took care of me, like a mama does, so she's my stepmom."

A lightbulb went off in Finley's head and he smiled. "Oh! Like Sam. I didn't know Sam was my stepmom." Sam's mouth opened and closed as she struggled to catch up with his three-year-old thought process.

"No, buddy, I'm not your stepmom."

"But mama loves you and you take care of me just like a mama. That's like a stepmom, right?" Sam's heart warmed at his words.

"Sort of, buddy, except me and your mama aren't married. So, it's a little different."

Finley shrugged. He got up off the table, the conversation clearly over for him as his toys beckoned. He ran toward the playroom and paused, looking over his shoulder.

"Well, when you and Mama get married, then you'll be my stepmom."

Sam's mouth dropped open again as she scrambled for what to say, but Finley was gone before she found any words. Brooke looked just as shocked. Lexi laughed.

"Kids, eh? So how long have you two been together?" Once again, Sam was at a loss for words. *Lexi thought they were together?* She'd told Lexi she was gay at their first lunch. She got it out of the way pretty quickly, not wanting to go any further if it was going to be a problem. Luckily, it wasn't. Lexi's roommate was a lesbian and one of her closest friends was transgender. She was clear on her acceptance immediately.

"We're not—well, we're just friends," Sam blurted. Lexi looked suitably embarrassed.

"Oh! I'm sorry. I just assumed."

Brooke smiled at Lexi and shook her head. "Don't worry about it. Seriously. It happened all the time in college, didn't it, Sam? That's what happens when you have two queer women who are best friends. It even happened when my husband was with us, luckily, he didn't care."

Lexi laughed as Sam willed her face to change from the beetroot colour she was sure it currently sported. "And your husband…" Lexi asked hesitantly. Although Sam had spoken to Lexi at length recently, with the weirdness between her and Brooke, she had avoided a lot of the harder topics.

"He passed away when Finley was a baby. Sam has been a constant support for us, but especially since Jake died. She's the best."

Sam shrugged and looked at Brooke, who stared back at her with eyes full of pure gratitude.

"Well, how else would I survive? I need you around to feed me." The napkin that flew at her head was Brooke's response to that.

❖

The rest of the lunch went great, despite Finley's outburst. Brooke really liked Lexi. She was happy for Sam. Her sister seemed to be a welcome addition to her life. It surprised Brooke to see Sam so open with someone who had the potential to hurt her.

Brooke left them to chat for a while under the guise of going to check on Finley. She needed to talk to him anyway. As they sat to play with his doll house in the playroom, she tried to approach it as naturally as possible.

"Fin, you know Sammy is my friend, yes?" He nodded, too engrossed in his imaginary world to look up.

"Sammy will always be our family, but not your stepmom, okay?" At that, his head perked up.

"Why not?"

Brooke sighed. How do you have a conversation about relationships with a three-year-old? Why did she even bother, he'd have forgotten if she just let it go.

"We aren't in a relationship. Your mama and daddy were in love and we got married and had you. Sam and I are friends."

Finley frowned, clearly unhappy with the explanation. "You don't love Sammy?" He crossed his arms as the lines that creased his forehead deepened.

"Of course I do." Brooke knew she had dug herself into a deeper hole.

"You love Sammy. Sammy love you. I love you and Sammy. We're a family. Nana says that love makes a family. You should talk to Nana."

Brooke laughed. That was the last thing that she should do. But she couldn't fault the kid's logic. "You're right, buddy, we are all a family. It's just a different type of love. It's a little complicated."

Finley rolled his eyes. Wonder where he got that from, Brooke thought to herself. She got up and walked back out to the kitchen where Lexi and Sam were engrossed in conversation. From the snippets she could hear, the topic moved on to their mother, or lack of.

"I tried looking for her but no luck. I'm not sure if that's a good thing or a bad thing." Lexi shrugged as Sam reached for her hand.

"Well, despite her faults, she made pretty awesome kids, right?" Brooke interjected, smiling as she placed her hand on Sam's shoulder.

"True that. We rock."

Brooke laughed at Sam, modest as always.

After many cups of tea and in-depth conversation, Lexi got up to go. Brooke smiled as they hugged after saying their goodbyes. When Lexi left, Sam came in and wrapped her arms around Brooke, hugging her tightly.

"Not that I'm complaining but what's this for?" Sam just held her for a few more moments before pulling back.

"For being you. For suggesting this, for the wonderful lunch, for making Lexi feel so at ease. Just…for everything."

The heat crept up Brooke's cheeks as a grin tugged at her mouth. She shook her head and turned so Sam wouldn't see how much her words meant. They tidied up together in peaceful silence and then spent the evening colouring and reading books with Finley. Sam stayed again that night. As she left for work the next morning Brooke wished the weekend didn't have to end.

She had taken the week off to be with Finley at home while he got used to the cast. He would have to go back to crèche eventually, but she wasn't ready yet. They had a lazy morning and then got ready to surprise Sam with lunch at work. The kid was a great excuse. It wasn't that she missed Sam after only the morning. Not at all.

They picked up food at one of their favourite places, then got to the store and asked the teenager at the counter for Sam. She seemed more than happy to get away from the computer. The sky was clear as they entered the park and Brooke laid out a blanket for them to picnic on. Not long after they arrived, she was watching Sam make daisy chains with Finley when they heard a familiar voice.

"Hey there."

Brooke looked up and who walked toward them but Dani and Ruby. Of course. Brooke tried to keep her face neutral as she looked at Ruby, but her smile for Dani was genuine. Even if it hadn't worked out, she really liked the other woman.

"Hey!"

Sam's reply was a little too enthusiastic for Brooke's liking.

"Fancy seeing you two here. Lunch date?" Dani enquired as Brooke started to blush. Would Dani say something in front of Sam? What was the deal with Sam and Ruby anyway? They had avoided the topic since the night at the bar, but maybe Ruby had looked Sam up or something. Social media made it easy to find people, right? Brooke felt so far out of the loop.

Finley ran up and plopped himself into Sam's lap before either woman could reply.

"Yes, we surprised Sammy with lunch." Finley took it upon himself to answer and they smiled down at him. "You must be Finley. I've heard so much about you. I hope your hand is feeling better after your superhero stunts."

Finley's smile widened at Dani's words and he nodded. "Yeah, lots better. Mama and Sammy gave me ice cream and we watched movies and then it was all better."

"I'm sure it was nice to have your mom and Sam there." Ruby smiled at Finley and he nodded back as her gaze switched to Sam.

Dani cleared her throat and gestured to the walkway. "We better get going, we're meeting some friends for lunch." They headed back toward the path and Brooke stared at Sam who watched them go.

"You gonna tell me what that was all about?"

Brooke shook out of her daze at Sam's words. "What?"

"Dani. The back and forth not so subtle glances. What's going on?"

Brooke shrugged. She should probably tell Sam. Or she should encourage her to go talk to Ruby. Ruby could be really good for Sam. But before she said anything, Sam continued. "A client of mine gifted me tickets to a concert this week. That I totally didn't forget about. Do you want to ask Maddie to watch Finley and come with me?"

Brooke hesitated. Sam's music taste could vary widely. "I'm agreeing to nothing until I know who."

Sam's smile was mischievous. "Just because you said that, I'm not telling you. You'll have to trust me and take your chances. Come on, it'll be fun. Just the two of us."

Brooke's heart fluttered. It wasn't a date. They had gone to many concerts together over the years. But the way Sam looked at her, twinkle in her eye as a smile curved her lips, it sure felt like she was asking her out. Brooke swore a swarm of butterflies took over her stomach as she took a deep breath. Date or not…there was only one answer that swam around her head.

"I'm in."

CHAPTER SEVENTEEN

An hour into the drive, Sam could see Brooke's restless shuffling in the passenger seat.

"How far away is this concert?"

This time, it was Sam who rolled her eyes. "Just like the last time I told you, not far. About ten more minutes."

"Do I at least get a hint?"

Sam was about to rebuff Brooke's attempts to get her to spill when a large billboard became visible on the side of the road they drove down. She couldn't stop the laugh that escaped. "Um, yeah, a pretty big hint."

As Brooke took in the advertisement, her eyes widened. "Seriously? We're going to see the Spice Girls?"

Sam's smile grew wider. Brooke had never gotten into the Spice Girls phase, but Sam had worshiped them. When she was a kid, girl power meant a lot more to her than just silly songs and dance routines. No, it meant possibilities. It meant power, which she had very little of while in foster care.

Sam waited for further complaints to come. When she was met with silence instead of the sarcastic comments or exasperated sighs she expected, she glanced over and took in Brooke's smile.

"What?"

"Nothing. I'll go rock out to the Spice Girls with you." Brooke reached out and pushed a stray lock of hair behind Sam's ear.

"It's not exactly a rock out kind of concert, but we can certainly spice up our lives." Brooke rolled her eyes as Sam grinned at her own pun. Business as usual.

Except, Sam couldn't stop thinking about everything. She had feelings for Brooke, she knew that. She tried for a long time to ignore them, but it became almost impossible since they'd slept together. She could happily spend every day of her life with Brooke and Fin. It was her fear of rejection that got in her way.

The part she kept thinking about was how she had let her feelings make her act in ways she would never usually act. She had treated Brooke badly. Awfully. She knew Brooke forgave her, but she hadn't forgiven herself for everything she said and did in her apartment that day.

She wasn't sure she was ready to do anything about her feelings. She didn't want to get hurt, and she didn't want to lose Brooke. But if she kept pushing Brooke away, she would lose her anyway. In the worst possible way. Because of her own fear and doubt. She had lost many relationships in her life for the same reason but none that meant as much to her as the woman sitting beside her.

Sam pulled into the car park for the concert and snapped out of her thoughts. The place was packed already. They went into the arena and browsed the merchandise stalls. Sam spent far too long trying to decide whether to buy a T-shirt or not that Brooke eventually just bought one for her. They got drinks and took their seats. Sam was really excited, and Brooke looked amused.

The concert was everything the little girl in Sam would have adored. Every time Sam looked over at Brooke, she was watching Sam. She spent most of the concert amused at Sam's reactions rather than the people on stage. They sang, laughed, danced, and had one of the best nights of Sam's life.

As they walked toward the exit at the end of the night, Sam turned to Brooke with the biggest smile on her face. Brooke shook her head and grinned. The place was packed so they were moving slowly.

"What?" Brooke shrugged but Sam continued, "Why are you looking at me like that?"

Brooke's hand grasped hers and her thumb moved over Sam's knuckles gently. "Happy looks good on you." Before Sam had too much time to think about it, Brooke continued, "But seriously, how did I not remember that Spice Girls songs were pure filth? No wonder you like them."

Sam laughed as they finally reached the exit and made their way outside. The weather was awful; rain poured down around them. Typical Irish weather, the sun shone on the drive here and now they were soaked to the skin in the few seconds it took just to run across the parking lot.

As Sam turned the key in the ignition with shaky hands, the engine sputtered and died. She tried again and again and nothing. The cold had already begun to creep in and she longed for the blast of warm air from the heater to come to life.

"This is unfortunate."

Sam raised an eyebrow and looked at Brooke. "Ya think?"

She grabbed her phone and dialled the breakdown service. After she explained where they were, the operator advised it might be hours before someone got to them. The weather, which had taken a nosedive since they entered the concert, meant lots of accidents. Traffic from the concert already piled up on the road in front of them. It was late; they were both tired and had no desire to wait hours for a breakdown service in soaked through clothes.

When Sam got off the phone she turned to Brooke. "What are our options here?"

"We could grab a taxi home, but it'll cost a fortune, and we'd have to drive back up here tomorrow to get your car."

Sam didn't like the sound of that.

"Tomorrow is funfair day. We promised Finley."

Brooke laughed. They both knew damn well Sam was looking forward to it just as much as Finley. If Fin's cast wasn't going to keep them from going, a little car trouble wouldn't stop Sam.

"The breakdown service said they'll tow it to the local mechanic, so we don't need to wait around. We could get a room here and pick it up there in the morning. Then we'd still make it home in plenty of time for the fair, assuming it's nothing major."

Sam shivered from the cold of the evening plus her rain drenched clothes.

"I think I better ring Maddie and tell her we won't be getting home tonight." Brooke picked up her phone and rang as Sam googled nearby hotels. Luckily, there was a hotel around the corner from them with one room left. She gulped at the exorbitant price, but had it booked before Brooke even got off the phone. The perks of modern technology.

They ran to the hotel and were absolutely soaked by the time they got into reception. After they checked in and got the key card, they headed up to the room, both visibly shivering by then. They key card clicked and unlocked the door which she pushed open. Sam's eyes immediately landed on the king-sized bed. Her heart started to beat faster, which she knew was ridiculous. They'd shared a bed many times before. But no matter how much she told herself it was the same as any other time, her heart kept up its steady rhythm.

"We need to get out of these clothes."

Sam realized after blurting it out how it sounded. Brooke grinned, but luckily didn't comment. Her teeth chattered as they stepped inside the small, but thankfully warm, hotel room.

"Um…what exactly are we going to wear?"

The thought seemed to cross both their minds at the same time because Brooke's eyes went wide. They weren't prepared for an overnight trip.

Sam ran to the bathroom, hoping against hope the hotel was nice enough to provide bathrobes. It sure had cost enough for them. Luckily, she spied two hung up on the back of the bathroom door and grabbed them, returning to a very flustered looking Brooke.

"We better get changed. We wouldn't want another fever situation."

Brooke's cheeks flamed as Sam laughed and walked into the bathroom.

❖

Brooke sat on the bed, flicking through the room service menu, when Sam walked out of the bathroom. If possible, Sam looked even more beautiful in the simple white, terrycloth robe than she had in the jeans and shirt she wore for the concert. Brooke was all too aware that Sam was almost certainly naked under the robe, considering her own underwear had been much too wet to leave on.

"Fancy something to eat?"

Sam nodded and joined her on the bed to look. They ordered food and scrolled through the channels on the TV as they waited for it to be delivered. They chose a random old movie and sat back, both pretending to be engrossed in it so as not to acknowledge the tension that had been building all night, even before they were close to naked on a bed together.

Brooke moved to get comfortable and her hand brushed up against Sam's. She stilled. Her breath hitched as Sam's thumb stroked her hand, gently back and forth. Eyes still on the television, Brooke inched her hand closer. Sam continued her movements and then entwined her fingers with Brooke's as her thumb still worked a path along Brooke's hand.

Brooke's stomach flip flopped. Sam affected her so profoundly with simply holding her hand. Her eyes fluttered closed, and Sam's body shifted closer to her. She needed to say something, anything, but her mouth was dry. Unlike other more southern parts of her body. *Since when had hand holding become such a turn-on?* She opened her eyes and turned her head toward Sam as she willed her mouth to finally speak.

"Sam, I—"

A knock on the door interrupted her, followed by a voice that announced their room service had arrived. She let out a frustrated breath and swore there was a hint of a smile on Sam's face as she jumped up to open the door. That, and an unmistakable flare of lust.

As the attendant wheeled the cart with food into the room, Brooke took a minute to gather her composure. The food looked wonderful. She would relax, enjoy a meal and the movie, and get her shit together.

They ate in silence. Brooke was sure the food was lovely, but she barely tasted a thing. Once they finished, Sam took the plates and placed them on the tray, then returned and muted the television.

"I think we need to talk."

Despite the fact that this was the mature thing to do, part of her felt like running away or burying her head in the pillows. Instead, she nodded.

"I think we were naive. That night when…" Sam teetered off and Brooke took over for her.

"When we had amazing hot sex and tried to pretend it meant nothing?"

Sam gulped and nodded. "Yeah. That. Exactly."

Brooke blew out a breath and shook her head. "Look, Sam, I'm attracted to you. That's pretty obvious. And I'm pretty sure you're attracted to me."

She paused a second as Sam nodded her confirmation, her eyes being all the proof Brooke needed.

"I'm worried. You're my best friend. I don't want to destroy everything we have. But I think we can both say that ignoring this hasn't worked. So, what do we do?"

Sam's eyes raked up and down Brooke's body which made it clear she had a few ideas. Sam leaned in toward her, giving Brooke an opportunity to move away before pressing their lips together. Brooke melted into the kiss and remembered how good Sam was at this. She reached up to cup Sam's cheek as Sam moved closer.

The kiss got heated quickly as they poured all the passion they had held back into it. As Sam's bare thigh brushed hers, Brooke groaned against her mouth and stilled her movements.

"Sam. Wait."

Sam pulled back and a look passed over her face.

"No, not like last time. I'm not stopping this. But we can't just jump back into sex and not talk about what this means."

Sam moved her hand to hold Brooke's again. "What do you want this to mean?"

Brooke had no idea how to answer that question. She had to say something, but what?

"I honestly don't know. I'm terrified, Sam. I'm afraid that this is going to be a huge mistake and I'll lose you. I can't lose you. Fin can't lose you."

Sam squeezed her hand. "Finley will never lose me. That will never happen. Do you understand?" Brooke nodded, and Sam continued, "I could tell you that you'll never lose me, but that is a risk. All of this is a risk. I don't know how I feel about that. But I do know how I feel about you, and I can't deny it anymore. I want you, B. I can't promise this is a good idea. But maybe if we take this day by day, we can figure it out along the way, together."

Together. Brooke liked the sound of that.

"Day by day. What about tonight?"

They should probably take a step back. Maybe go on a date. Take it slowly. That would be the smart idea.

"We could take this slow, go to sleep now, and talk more in the morning. Or…"

"Or?"

"Or we could take tonight as a break from reality, get the tension out of our systems, and start fresh tomorrow."

Brooke didn't need any more encouragement than that. She liked whatever option got Sam naked and moaning beneath her best. They kissed again, and there was no holding back this time. The robes got discarded soon after, and Brooke lost her breath all over again at Sam's body in all its glorious beauty.

"You're just…wow."

Sam kissed her softly and whispered in her ear, "I feel exactly the same about you."

Brooke had a moment where everything felt so strange. This was Sam. Her Sam, her best friend Sam. Except it wasn't. It was more. This was Sam who looked at her like she was the most beautiful woman in the world. Like she wanted nothing more than to worship her body. The body that had stretch marks from her pregnancy. That she critiqued in the morning when she got ready in front of her floor length mirror. The body that to her was just regular.

In Sam's eyes, she was extraordinary. Sam pushed her onto her stomach and started to trail her lips from Brooke's neck down her back and Brooke knew that worshiping her body was exactly what Sam was going to do.

Sam traced circles between her legs before she pressed two fingers inside her from behind. Brooke already ached for Sam. She arched back into her touch and gripped the bedsheets as Sam quickened her pace. Sam pressed her lips to Brooke's shoulder blade and bit lightly, before two final strokes made Brooke's legs clench as immense pleasure rippled through her body. Sam moved to lie beside her and curled against her as she peppered light kisses along Brooke's shoulder.

"I love watching you come undone."

Sam's whispered words sent shivers down Brooke's spine. She turned to face Sam and ran a finger down her cheek.

"I love when you make me come undone."

Brooke kissed Sam's lips and then traced a line along her jaw until she reached her earlobe. She nibbled and sucked as Sam's breath picked up and she rolled onto her back, pulling Brooke on top.

Brooke's lips trailed down farther, nibbling on Sam's neck as Sam's fingers tangled in her hair.

"Fuck, B. More."

Brooke licked, sucked, and bit the crook of Sam's neck while she moved her hand down between Sam's legs. Sam was already soaked and ready for her. Brooke groaned and plunged a finger inside her, soon she added a second and pumped in and out fast, matching Sam's pace.

It didn't take long before Sam called her name and clenched around her fingers. Brooke was sure it was the sexiest thing she had ever seen. As Sam came back down to earth, Brooke kissed a path down her stomach. When she reached her destination, Sam whimpered. Brooke looked up.

"Are you okay?"

Sam nodded, blatant, unbridled desire all over her face.

"More than. I just came, and I'm aching for you already. How can you do this to me?"

Brooke felt the exact same way if the damp between her legs was anything to go by. "I have no idea, but you better get used to it."

Sam moaned at that and pushed her fingers back into Brooke's hair. Brooke smiled before she lost herself between Sam's legs, bringing her to bliss once more.

CHAPTER EIGHTEEN

Sam woke the next morning and took a moment before she opened her eyes, hoping last night hadn't been a very elaborate dream. The weight of the arm around her naked body assured her that it wasn't.

She peeked her eyes open and smiled. Brooke was still asleep, faced toward her, one arm flung over her and the other above her head. She drooled adorably, and her hair was a mess, as it always was first thing in the morning.

Sam took time to look at her. She couldn't help but wonder how she went this long without acknowledging the depth of her feelings. Her heart was so full as she studied Brooke's face. It was so beautiful, drool and all.

Brooke fluttered her eyes open and caught Sam staring. Busted. Sam's breath caught as a grin lit up Brooke's face.

"Watching me sleep, Sammy? Not creepy at all."

Sam shrugged. "What can I say? The drool does it for me."

Brooke rolled her eyes and wiped at her mouth as Sam laughed. Sam sobered as Brooke's thigh pushed between her legs.

She arched against it automatically, and she leaned in to press her mouth against Brooke's when her phone started to ring. They both groaned audibly, but Sam reached for it, aware it was likely the breakdown service. They said they'd ring in the morning with an update.

She spoke for a few minutes and found out that her car had been towed to a garage about a ten-minute walk from the hotel, and was ready to be picked up. Luckily, it had been a quick fix. That, plus the damage it would do to her credit card was about as much as she took in considering she knew nothing about cars.

She hung up and stretched. Brooke had slipped out of the bed and gone to the bathroom during the call. She returned wearing way too many clothes for Sam's liking. Brooke rolled her eyes as she caught Sam's pout.

"We have to hit the road. Somebody promised Finley we would go to the funfair later today."

Sam jumped up out of bed, suddenly excited. The traveling funfair came to town this time every year, and this was the first year Finley would properly enjoy it. They had been excited about this for weeks.

Brooke's eyes travelled the length of her naked body.

"How long is the funfair here for again?"

Sam shook her head, grabbing her now dry underwear from the radiator to pull them on. "Don't even think about it, B. Finley knows we're going today. No rescheduling."

It was Brooke's turn to pout. "Don't pretend this is all about Fin. You're more excited than he is."

As Sam got dressed, she nodded. "True. But who could blame me? Rides, games, prizes, cotton candy. I love the funfair."

Sam walked into the bathroom to brush her teeth with the complimentary travel kit reception had given them last night.

"I can think of a few games we can play right here. Rides too."

Sam poked her head out of the bathroom at Brooke's words and raised her eyebrows. Brooke put her face in her hands.

"Don't say it. I know. That was awful."

Sam finished up in the bathroom and walked out, shaking her head slowly. "It was worse than awful. Terrible. I think I may need some time to recover from that statement before I can look at you again."

Brooke swatted her ass and pulled Sam in, lips pressed against hers in a chaste kiss. "You sure about that?"

Sam gulped. Brooke was not playing fair. She leaned in and captured Brooke in another, more heated kiss. Hands moved to her hips as they backed against the wall and that thigh was placed firmly between her legs again.

She pulled back and looked at Brooke. Breathing heavy, eyes filled with desire and lips swollen already. She could barely comprehend everything she was feeling, but one thing was for sure. There was nowhere else she would rather be.

"Maybe we can be a little late."

Two hours later, Brooke spoke to Maddie on the walk to the garage. She relayed to Sam how she got the third degree from a very excited Finley. He was concerned about the funfair, dressed since eight a.m. as he waited impatiently for them. Once they were in the car and on the way home, they still made good time, despite the later-than-planned start.

Guilt panged until she remembered Brooke's head between her legs as she gripped the wall and the guilt seemed less important. They were still going to have lots of fun at the fair, just a little later than usual. It was about time Brooke put herself first anyway. Sam just helped her with that process.

"So…should we talk?"

As Sam focused on Brooke's words, she knew that realistically they had to. Being away in the hotel for the night had been a break from reality. All the reasons why doing this hadn't been a good idea had seemed irrelevant. But those reasons still existed and needed to be discussed. Sam just wasn't sure she was ready to face the world outside of this little bubble they had created.

"Yeah, we should, but…not now? Can we just have a day at the funfair with Fin and enjoy ourselves before we talk about what everything means?"

Sam bit her lip and waited for Brooke to reply. After a few minutes, Brooke simply nodded her agreement and cranked up the music. They sailed the rest of the way home dancing along to the carefree sounds of summer love on the radio.

❖

Ten minutes after they arrived at the funfair, Brooke shook her head at the level of excitement coming from her two companions. She wasn't sure who was worse, Sam or Finley. Sam grabbed their hands and pulled them toward the bumper cars. Scratch that, it was definitely Sam.

A year after they met, when Brooke found out Sam had never been to a funfair, she had to change that. She would never forget the pure excitement and wonder on Sam's face that first time. And every single year since.

The broken arm incident had thrown a spanner in the works and they had gone back and forth as to whether they should still go. Brooke checked and Fin could still do most of the things geared to his age, and the cast certainly hadn't held him back from running circles around them at home, so here they were. And there was that look again that made Sam's face light up and the butterflies in Brooke's stomach try to break free.

They queued up as Finley held both their hands and practically vibrated with glee. Sam looked at Brooke over her shoulder with a giddy smile that melted Brooke's heart. The wink that followed melted other parts of her anatomy.

They had been very careful since collecting Finley. No hand holding, no remarks, strictly friends. Until they had time to discuss this, they agreed they couldn't confuse him. It didn't stop the memories from the night before racing through Brooke's head every time Sam glanced at her a certain way, or licked her lips, or brushed up against her in passing.

The brushing up against her was no accident, Brooke was sure. The small smiles that played on the side of Sam's lips gave it away. Brooke snapped out of her daydream as they neared the top of the line. Sam stared at her, eyebrow raised. A look on Sam's face said she knew exactly what was on Brooke's mind.

"It's our turn! It's our turn!"

Finley bounced up and down as he reached the top of the queue. Once advised, he darted to the bright red car with an orange streak along its side. It was two per car. Brooke slipped in beside Finley, and Sam claimed the green car behind them. Game on.

The music blared as the cars started, and immediately there was a thud behind them. Finley's eyes went round. "She hit us, Mama!"

Brooke laughed at his outrage and grabbed the wheel to spin around, playing chase with Sam as she laughed. "Yeah, buddy, that's the point of the game. Now we go hit her."

Finley's giggles could be heard miles off when they finally caught up with Sam and bumped into her. A few minutes after it started, the cars slowed as it ended, and Finley begged to go again. With promises of lots more games ahead and another go before they left, he exited the car without tears.

Next was the fun house. As they wove their way around, Brooke hung back to watch Sam help Finley in and out of all the obstacles and make silly faces in the mirrors. She was struck by how right everything was. Being here with her son and her…what? Best friend? Always. Girlfriend? Too soon…right? But that's where this was leading if last night was anything to go by.

When Brooke brought it up in the car earlier, Sam didn't seem too thrilled to discuss it. Brooke knew it was likely fear, as it was for her. Were they overthinking it, making it more complicated than it needed to be? Right now, she could never imagine anything happening to tear them apart for good. Then again, she hadn't imagined that about her and Jacob, either. But it wasn't like she'd have been any less devastated if something like that had happened to Sam a week ago. She had always been, and still was her person.

"Look at this giant slide, Mama!"

Finley reached the top of the fun house and the huge tube slide that led to the bottom. Brooke was worried about his arm, but Sam agreed to take him down. Brooke ran to the bottom, camera readied on her phone. She snapped a photo of them with the biggest smiles just as they came out at the end. Another photo was taken as Sam tried, and failed, to get up off the floor.

"A little help would be nice," Sam grumbled. Brooke laughed and lent her a hand. The electricity that sparked through her fingers just from that simple touch made Brooke's breath hitch. If Sam's pupils were an indicator, Brooke wasn't the only one who felt it. If they hadn't been in the presence of her toddler, she wouldn't have been able to stop herself from pulling Sam close and kissing her senseless. For now, she simply ran her thumb along Sam's hand and pulled away reluctantly.

The rest of the day was spent going on all the rides that Finley was allowed on and back on the bumper cars as promised. This time, Sam and Finley teamed up to get Brooke, and his excited exclamations when they bumped into her turned Brooke's smile to laughter. After that, they went for cotton candy. It was Finley's first time tasting it, and his eyes went wide as it melted in his mouth. After the few bites he was allowed, there was more stuck to his face than what he had consumed. They took photos and played games, and Sam even won a teddy which Finley claimed.

"One last ride before we go, buddy. How about the Ferris wheel?"

Finley's eyes followed Brooke's pointed finger. "Whoa!"

His eyes were as big as saucers as he took in the giant wheel that rotated ahead of them. He nodded apprehensively, and they walked toward it. As they clambered into a passenger car and started to move, Finley clung to her leg. As it got higher, Sam coaxed him over to the side to look out at the views. He soon got a bit braver and started to point things out.

"Look at those teeny cars!"

As they got higher and higher, he yelled about how small everything had gotten. Brooke joined them at the edge, wrapping one arm around each of them from behind. It was such a natural thing to do and one she wouldn't have questioned a few weeks ago. But now…was it okay? Sam's hand landed on hers at her waist and held it tight against her, answering her unspoken question.

Finley chattered the whole way back to the car about everything they had done that day. Two minutes after they left the funfair, he snored in his car seat. Brooke smiled as she looked at her son in the mirror. "I think we wore him out."

Sam hummed her agreement. The day had been long and tiring but so worth it. Days like this were the ones Brooke wanted to think of in times when things got hard. She would pull these memories up and calm herself when stress took over.

Sam reached for her hand and held it. "I had a great day today, B."

Brooke squeezed her hand and sighed happily. "Me too, Sammy." Sam yawned then, and Brooke laughed. "You'll be joining Finley when your head hits the couch cushion. Are you, um, staying tonight?"

Sam glanced at her then back to the road. "Do you want me to?"

Brooke stopped herself before she blurted out the first thing that came to her head. She never wanted her to leave.

"Yeah. We can just watch a movie and get an early night. We're both tired, there's no point in you driving home when you have date day with Finley tomorrow."

Brooke wanted to assure Sam that she didn't expect anything, without having to actually say it. Sam was silent until they reached the house. She carried Finley inside and to his bed as Brooke stripped off his pants and let him sleep in underwear and a T-shirt.

"So, could we skip the movie and just go straight to the bed part?"

Brooke nodded at Sam's words. "Sure, I know you're tired. I'll see you in the morning?"

Sam's hand slipped into hers as the fingers on her other hand pushed Brooke's chin up to look into her eyes. "I think you misunderstood me. I meant…I want to go to bed with you."

Brooke pulled Sam toward her and kissed her deeply. She whispered against her lips, "Are you sure? You were practically falling asleep in the car. We don't have to…"

Sam cut her off as her tongue traced over Brooke's jaw and up to her earlobe. She licked and sucked as Brooke whimpered, then whispered softly, "Take me to bed, B."

CHAPTER NINETEEN

Sam woke the next morning wrapped in Brooke again. She could definitely get used to this. They both wore T-shirts, having remembered to put them on last night to avoid any unnecessary conversations when Finley made his appearance. Brooke's bare thigh was against her own, though, and even that margin of skin-on-skin contact was enough to send her mind to the gutter.

She held Brooke a little tighter, but from the light that peeked through curtains, it likely wouldn't be long before they were interrupted by Finley. So, despite the pulse between her legs, Sam didn't want to start anything they couldn't finish.

Her head swam with so many thoughts and feelings. Being with Brooke like this was everything she ever wanted. Not just the physical side, although that was off the charts. Better than anything she had ever experienced before. More than that, this thing with Brooke could be amazing in every aspect. But could she put aside her fear, her past and take the leap? Brooke already had the ability to break her heart. If they took this next step, made it official, and it didn't work out, she could obliterate it.

Brooke stirred against her, and Sam knew she didn't have much of a choice either way. There was no chance she would walk away from Brooke now. She couldn't live with the *what might have been*. She just had to find a way to get over her fear, so she didn't ruin this before it even began. She had to open up to Brooke and let her know the worries in her head.

She trusted Brooke more than anyone in the world. So, if Brooke felt the same, she had to trust that they would figure it out. And that was the big question: how did Brooke feel? There was only one way to find out, and she was both ready and terrified for that conversation.

Brooke wouldn't have taken the risk of the past couple days unless she had strong feelings for Sam. But her old insecurities still raged, and she couldn't shut them off. The feelings of never being good enough or wanted enough. Her last therapist would have had a lot to say about her abandonment issues. It was probably time enough to give her another call and tackle them head on instead of her usual avoidance techniques.

Brooke's eyes opened and a lazy smile stretched across her face. "This watching me sleep thing is becoming a habit."

Sam couldn't stop her own smile if she tried. She found herself leaning in as she brushed her lips against Brooke's softly. Cupping Brooke's face in her hand, she stared at her some more. "It's my new favourite hobby."

"You know we need to talk about all of this right?"

Sam nodded at Brooke's words but couldn't even think of how to start. They needed time and privacy to talk it all through. The pitter patter of pre-schooler feet coming across the hallway indicated they weren't going to get that right now.

"Tonight?"

Brooke nodded in response as Sam dropped her eyes to Brooke's full lips, contemplating if she had time for one more kiss. Brooke lifted her chin with one hand, curling their pinkie fingers together with the other and whispered, "Tonight."

Finley jumped onto the bed as Sam gulped from the look that had just been in Brooke's eyes. Promises of much more than just a kiss later. She focused her attention on the here and now with a heart full of hope.

Fin was super excited that Sam was still here and cuddled in between them. They spent another hour telling stories and singing off-key songs. As Sam tickled him, and his laughter rang through the room with Brooke smiling at her over his mop of brown curls, she couldn't help but think of how perfect it was.

When Fin finally nagged them out of bed, Sam got dressed and ready for their date. This week was a brunch date at a buffet. Finley couldn't believe that he was going to get to eat as much as he wanted of whatever he wanted. Especially when he found out there was a whole section of serve your own ice cream.

Just as they were about to head out the door, Brooke called Sam back. "How about after you finish your date with the kiddo, we have a date of our own?"

Brooke looked nervous; her hands fidgeted as she said it. Sam glanced around to make sure Finley wasn't near and leaned in, brushing a soft kiss across Brooke's lips, lingering just a little bit.

"I would love to go on a date with you, Brooke."

Brooke grinned and shooed them out the door with a grumble about the errands she had to run while they were off having fun. Her wink had Sam's heart flipping all the way to the restaurant.

❖

After they left, Brooke paced the house. She asked Sam on a date. Sam said yes. What did that mean? Did it mean they were dating? Is that what Brooke wanted? Nerves, fear, and excitement zipped through her body in a confused mess of anxiousness. They would have to talk about all of this, probably tonight, but first, she had a date to plan.

She racked her mind trying to think of what to do. Fancy dinner? That had never been their type of thing. Cinema? Good for possible make out sessions but not so great for talking. By the contemplative look on Sam's face when Brooke woke this morning, she clearly had a lot on her mind. They needed to discuss this before Sam talked herself out of it. Brooke might not know exactly what she wanted, but it wasn't that.

She rang Maddie to see if she'd watch Finley, and she was more than happy to. Brooke worried about having to ask too often lately, but Maddie soon shut her up about that, complaining that she didn't get enough time with him as it was. With a babysitter sorted, they were free to go wherever they wanted, but her mind was blank.

She spent the rest of the afternoon getting caught up on housework and not getting any further on the date front. This should be easy, right? They did stuff together all the time, and she never had trouble deciding then. But everything she thought of was just…regular. She wanted this to be special.

Sam dropped Finley off after the buffet and went back to her apartment to get ready for the date that Brooke had yet to plan. She'd told Sam to keep it casual, that she would pick her up and that she'd message her when Maddie arrived.

Brooke and Finley spent the next couple of hours assembling his many jigsaws, painting each other's nails, colouring, and spending quality time together. He bragged excitedly about his day with Sam. The ice cream section was definitely a hit.

Brooke reminded him that they had the open day for his new pre-school the following evening. He would be starting there next month.

"Can Sammy come?" Finley looked up from his drawing as he spoke. "Please?" He added extra eyelid flutters as he drew out the plea in his sweetest voice.

"I'll ask, and if she doesn't have plans, I'm sure she'd love to come."

Finley smiled and got back to his drawing as Brooke mentally reminded herself to ask Sam later.

When Maddie arrived, Brooke was still no closer to a decision on what to do. Her brain kept hopping from one thing to another. She was tempted to ask Maddie her opinion, but was nowhere near ready to broach that conversation. Talking to her dead husband's sister about a date with her best friend? No, she'd skip that one for as long as possible.

She wasn't sure if Maddie would have a problem with it. From their conversation at her parents' house, she was encouraging Brooke to start to move on. And Brooke knew Maddie adored Sam.

But what if Maddie worried Brooke would forget Jacob? Brooke knew that wasn't true. A new relationship didn't negate what she and Jacob had, but Maddie was Jacob's sister. She was Brooke's sister now, too. Brooke wanted to make sure she knew nothing changed that.

How would Jacob's parents react? They were her family, and she adored them; she didn't want to do anything to jeopardize that. Realistically, she understood that they wouldn't want her to spend the rest of her life alone, but the reality could be very different when it happened.

She was lost in her own thoughts that spiralled into worry when Finley piped up to Maddie, "Mama and Sammy was kissing like that."

Brooke froze. She stared at Finley who gazed at the television, where an advertisement played as two actors kissed. Her best guess was something about perfume, but she was a little too distracted to pay attention. Her mind screamed for her to say something as Maddie looked at her with wide eyes. Finley had gone back to play right away as if he hadn't just dropped a bomb.

"Oh, really?"

Maddie quirked her head and posed her question at a stunned Brooke, but Finley took it upon himself to answer.

"Yup. Before date brunch. They is going on a date, too."

Brooke's hopes of making it out of this one without a conversation sank even further. How did he overhear that? Clearly, he had been paying more attention than either of them noticed.

Maddie got up and dragged Brooke into the kitchen. "So?"

A lie would only make it worse, Brooke knew that. She sighed. It was now or never.

"We kissed. I didn't realize Finley had seen us. We're going out tonight. I'm sorry if that's weird for—"

"It's about damn time."

Brooke wondered if she heard wrong but the smile on Maddie's face said otherwise. "What?"

"I've been waiting for you two to finally admit your feelings for each other. It's been plainly obvious to anyone with two eyes for the past few months."

Brooke shook her head and tried to arrange her thoughts. "Mads, I want you to know this doesn't change anything I had with Jacob."

Maddie rolled her eyes. "Why would it? You loved my brother as if the sun rose and set with him. I never questioned that. God knows why, but that bonehead was your world. Having feelings for Sam doesn't change how you felt about him, Brooke."

Although Brooke tried to tell herself the same thing daily, it sounded different coming from Maddie. More believable, understandable. She nodded and let a small smile play on her lips.

"I'm terrified. I have no idea what to do tonight."

Maddie's eyebrows rose. "You...don't know what to do?"

Brooke took a minute to process what Maddie implied and slapped her lightly on the arm. "Not like that, you perv. I asked Sam out on a date and now I have no idea what to actually do for the date."

"Of course you do, Brooke," Maddie laughed. "You've known Sam forever. You know everything she likes. Just stop thinking about this as if it must be some big grand gesture. What would make Sam smile?"

Brooke considered that for a minute. She remembered Sam in bed earlier that morning, smiling at her over Finley's head, how gorgeous she looked while telling Finley his favourite story.

Then it hit her.

"Maddie, you are a genius."

Maddie shrugged as if this was no new information to her. "Glad to be of service."

Brooke hesitated. "I should probably talk to Finley about all of this first, though."

Maddie shook her head. "Go. Enjoy your date. It's late, and he needs to get to bed soon anyway. You can talk to him tomorrow. Or avoid it forever like you were probably planning."

Brooke laughed and went to say goodbye to Finley. After promises about going to the library the next day, she texted Sam to say she left. She made a couple stops along the way to get what she needed and turned up at Sam's about thirty minutes later.

She knocked on the door, and her heart started to beat wildly. Was this a terrible idea? Was Sam going to expect something more romantic? The widened eyes and grin on Sam's face when she answered the door told Brooke that no, it was perfect. "Fancy staying in?"

Sam laughed and grabbed the pizza from her hand as Brooke followed her in and set the beer on the table. Sam's smile was all the reassurance she needed that she remembered the throwback to when their friendship truly began. Pizza and beer were enough to keep Sam in her life back then, and hopefully it would work its magic tonight.

CHAPTER TWENTY

After they polished off the pizza and one beer each while they talked and laughed, Sam's head and heart were lighter than she remembered being anytime recently. Everything was so normal, except infinitely different. Each touch lingered a little longer, the conversation held a hint more flirtation and each flicker of eyes to lips led to quick, stolen kisses and fluttering hearts. Sam was determined to enjoy this date and not simply hop into bed just because they stayed in.

When she opened the door to Brooke with the pizza and beer, it was surreal. They could've been back in college, everything hesitant and new again. That night was still one of the best she remembered in her life. It was the start of a new chapter, a better chapter, where she wasn't alone anymore. Though they had begun this next chapter of their story weeks ago with that night in bed together, this first date signified another beginning.

She wanted to talk and laugh and just be together. She also knew they had a lot to discuss. When her lips met Brooke's again during a gap in conversation, she almost gave up on the conversation altogether. She ran her hands over Brooke's clothed body. As she continued her exploration down past the curves that made her mouth water, she ached to rip the barriers off and feel Brooke's skin beneath her.

As she kissed her way down Brooke's neck, the throbbing between her legs intensified. Screw talking, right? Unfortunately, Brooke wasn't so easily distracted.

"What are we doing?"

Sam pulled back and looked Brooke in the eyes as she regained control of her breathing and grinned. "If you have to ask, I'm definitely not doing it right."

Brooke rolled her eyes. "I'm serious, Sammy. We clearly have amazing chemistry. The sex is...mind-blowing seems too tame. You're my best friend, and I love spending time with you. My son adores you. But what are we?"

Sam didn't know what to say. She knew what she wanted this to be. But was that a possibility?

"Honestly...I don't know. I agree with everything you said. But what happens if this doesn't work? How do we stop this from snowballing?"

They were already so close that it would be near impossible not to let this go too fast. Too much too soon might ruin them before they'd even begun.

"I don't have all the answers," Brooke began, "but clearly, ignoring this didn't work. Pretending it was nothing didn't work. Going back to just friends without even trying—I don't see how that's going to work. I look at you, and I imagine kissing you. I imagine my hands on your body, my lips on yours, you wrapped in my arms. I don't know how I could stop thinking those things. It's like I opened a door that I can't close again. At least until I see what's on the other side."

Sam nodded and warmth spread throughout her body. Even though she knew from Brooke's lips on hers that she wanted Sam, it was good to hear that she wanted more. Plus, Brooke was right. They owed it to themselves to see if this worked.

They didn't have much of a choice anyway. The attraction was building from the moment their lips met that first night, and they could deny it all they wanted, but ignoring it might very well be the thing that ruined their friendship.

"So...we try this?" Sam pointed back and forth between them.

Brooke nodded. "We try this. One day at a time. That's the only way we can stop it from becoming too much. Day by day, okay?"

Sam agreed, but had one question. An important one.

"What do we tell Fin? Do we just say nothing until we're sure of what this is?"

She didn't know if he'd even know what them dating meant, but after his stepmom comments, she didn't want to get his hopes up too soon.

Brooke gulped. Her gaze darted around before settling on Sam as she spoke. "Well, he kind of already knows something. And maybe, so does Maddie."

Sam's mouth fell open in shock. "What? What the hell, Brooke?"

She said it more in disbelief than anger.

"Don't blame me, Romeo. My crafty son somehow caught you laying one on me before you left for your date with him. He also heard us talk about tonight. He decided the best time to relay this information would be to Maddie when she arrived to babysit tonight."

Sam burst out laughing. Typical Finley. He had a habit of repeating things at the most inopportune times. Like when Brooke's mom visited, and he kept referring to her as Elsa. Which he happily explained to her was because Sam called her the Ice Queen, due to her inability to show affection to Brooke. He didn't say that last part, but by the look on Brooke's mom's face, she got it. That had gone over super well.

"So, what did you say to him?"

"Nothing, I ran out to our date. We'll need to talk to him tomorrow once we figure out what to say."

Sam's stomach dropped. "We?"

"Yes, we. You got us into this with your inability to keep your lips to yourself, so you're not getting away with it that easily."

"Oh, so you want me to keep my lips to myself?" Sam moved back to the other end of the couch. "Got it. I'll keep them all the way over here."

Sam followed Brooke's gaze as it moved towards her mouth. She was biting her lower lip in anticipation, fully aware of what the action would stir in Brooke. Her anticipation grew as Brooke's eyes got dark with lust. "Maybe just when the kid is around."

Brooke's eyes lingered on her lips as she moved closer.

"So where exactly do you want my lips right now?"

Sam could see the effect her words had on Brooke, and she loved it.

"Everywhere."

Brooke was on top of her, lips pressed against hers, and her body covered Sam's on the couch. The throbbing returned as Brooke's thigh made its way between her legs and grinded against her. She was so turned on already, and their clothes were still mostly intact.

"Brooke, bed, now."

Sam missed the weight of Brooke on her but was soon distracted by Brooke's hand in hers, pulling her up.

They almost made it to the bedroom before she had Brooke up against a wall, their lips crushed together once more. Sam couldn't wait; she needed Brooke right now. She unbuttoned Brooke's pants and helped her get out of them, underwear included, as she kissed anywhere she reached along the way.

She dropped to her knees as Brooke spread her legs with a whimper. She held Brooke back against the wall and licked a trail, tasting how wet Brooke was already. Brooke gasped and tangled her hand in Sam's hair, encouraging her further. Sam went to work bringing pleasure to Brooke. She led her to the peak and then changed positions, not quite letting Brooke reach her sought after destination. Brooke's moans turned to whimpers as she began to beg.

"Sam, please…I need you."

Sam smiled against her, loving the power she had in this position. Using one hand to hold Brooke in place, she moved the other and pushed two fingers inside Brooke while sucking on the spot that would be Brooke's undoing.

It only took a minute before Brooke's legs shook with the orgasm that rippled through her body. Sam stayed in place until the last waves subsided and then pulled back. Brooke sighed, slumping down as a smile flitted across her face.

Sam leaned in and kissed her softly. "You said everywhere."

❖

Brooke lay in Sam's bed, recovering from her third orgasm of the night. It must have been at least two in the morning, and she was sleepy. Sam's arms were around her, Brooke's head on her shoulder as Sam played with her hair absentmindedly.

"I wish we didn't have work tomorrow. We could just stay in bed and do this all day long."

"Mmm," Brooke muttered sleepily. Then she remembered she had something to ask Sam. "Do you have plans tomorrow evening?"

Sam raised an eyebrow. "That good, huh?"

Brooke huffed. "Get your mind out of the gutter. Finley's pre-school open night is tomorrow evening, and he wanted me to ask you to come."

Sam's eyebrow dropped as a genuine smile lit up her face. "Of course. I wouldn't miss it."

Brooke's heart skipped a beat, and an overwhelming rush of feelings encompassed her. How did she get so lucky? Not only did Sam rock her world in so many ways, she was genuinely excited to go to a school event for Brooke's kid. Something that most people would try to get out of made Sam smile like she'd just been offered a weeklong cruise in the Bahamas. Brooke shook her head.

Sam looked at her with a curious smile on her face. "What are you shaking your head at there, B?"

Their agreement of day by day meant not spilling her guts right here in this bed, on what was really only their first official date. If Brooke were to say what she was actually thinking, it would definitely constitute going too quick.

"Your adorableness, nerd. Of course you'd be excited to go to school."

Sam grinned. "Do you think they'll let me play with the blocks?"

Brooke expected nothing less than to see Sam do exactly that. Sam was always the first to get on the floor and play with Finley. Brooke was convinced most of the toys Sam bought him were really for herself. She loved the excuse to be a big kid, recapturing some of the youth she deserved. Brooke loved her for it.

Her heart squeezed at the idea. She loved Sam. She was her best friend, they'd been saying "I love you" to each other for years. But this was different, right? She couldn't say it here, lying in bed, naked. It wasn't the same context. Even with a heart so full that it might burst. She couldn't say it, but her body would.

Her sleepiness evaporated as she looked at Sam, the change in the mood written all over her face. She moved on top of Sam and kissed her slowly, tenderly. She pulled back and looked into Sam's eyes. The intensity almost overwhelmed her. Sam gulped as she softly whispered, the question in her voice evident, "Brooke?"

Brooke pressed her forehead against Sam's, and then she moved her tongue inside her mouth. The kiss started slowly and lingered as she enjoyed every second of it. Felt every part of it. Sam's hands wrapped around her and held her close, not pushing for more. She was happy to just be in this moment, kissing her like it was the most important thing in the world.

Brooke ran her hand down Sam's body, not breaking the kiss even for a moment. She moved to the side a little to allow her fingers a clear path to their destination. She started slowly, tenderly caressed every inch of heat between Sam's legs. Sam groaned against her mouth, their kisses broken with sighs as Brooke picked up the pace and moved her fingers inside Sam. As Sam's kisses grew frantic, Brooke pulled back and slowed her movements again.

"Kiss me," Sam requested.

Brooke shook her head. "I want to watch you come undone for me, baby."

Sam looked like she was ready to, just from Brooke's words.

As Brooke moved faster again, Sam's head arched back, and her eyes closed. Brooke stopped, her free hand moved to Sam's face and guided her head back up as her eyes flickered open.

"Eyes on me. I want to see everything I do to you. I want to see you want me."

Sam bit her lip and complied.

"I want you every minute of every day. So damn much."

Brooke moved back and rocked against Sam's thigh, looking into her eyes. Sam's eyes were wet with unshed tears, her emotions on display as Brooke led them both to the breaking point. She moved her hips faster on Sam's thigh as she matched the pace with her fingers, landing her palm at an angle that made Sam shudder with each thrust.

Brooke leaned down toward Sam, who met her halfway in a heart-stopping kiss as they both tumbled over the edge at the same time, clinging to each other. Sweating, panting and completely blissed out, they lay wrapped in each other's arms.

It wasn't long before Sam's soft snores greeted Brooke. She moved to the side and pulled Sam in close against her before kissing her forehead. She held her tight. Her heart couldn't possibly feel more than it did right in this moment. She stared at her person, the one who had been a constant in an ever-moving world and gave herself a moment to imagine that this was everything she would ever need.

She sighed, then allowed herself to say out loud what her body said for her. What Sam's eyes had said as Brooke stared into their depths. What was both the best and most terrifying thought she had had in a very long time.

"I love you."

CHAPTER TWENTY-ONE

The next morning, Sam stirred to the sound of a tornado in her room. Except, it was actually a Brooke-shaped hurricane rushing around.

"What time is it?" Sam grumbled.

"Six a.m." Brooke didn't pause from whatever she was doing.

"It's barely morning. What in the world are you up to?" Sam's eyes flickered open fully and focused on Brooke in the middle of getting dressed.

"I was trying to find my clothes that seem to have somehow gone everywhere. I'm robbing your socks."

Sam had difficulty keeping up. They stayed up until all hours devouring each other; it was past two in the morning the last time she checked the clock. Her eyes were gritty, and her mouth was dry.

"There's water on the locker," Brooke answered her unspoken question. Gratefully, Sam gulped down the fresh water that Brooke must have put there when she got up.

Sam was lucky that her job matched her tendency to avoid early mornings. She usually slept in a bit and started later. Her hours were pretty flexible when working for herself unless she had meetings or was under pressure for a client. The earliest she ever got up was the weekends she spent at Brooke's when the bundle of energy that was Finley demanded it.

She let her eyes land on Brooke as Brooke finished getting ready. She looked tired but happy. Her hair was a mess, but it still worked. Brooke always looked amazing.

"You sure you wanna rush out of here?"

Sam put on her best flirty voice and pulled the blankets back just a little, a hint of her bare thigh poking out from underneath. Brooke's eyes locked onto the creamy skin, and her tongue involuntarily licked her lips. Her eyes narrowed as she readjusted her gaze onto Sam's.

"Stop teasing. I need to get home before Fin wakes."

Sam pouted and traced her fingers over her own thigh as Brooke's eyes followed their path. "He won't be up till at least seven. Your place is only fifteen minutes from here…" She allowed her voice to trail off as her hand moved further under the blanket.

Brooke's eyes fluttered closed and she groaned. "Sam."

With that word, and the hunger in Brooke's eyes as they opened, Sam knew she would get her way. But that didn't mean she couldn't have fun teasing a little more.

Her fingers slipped between her legs and she let out a soft sigh. "It's okay, you can go, I can take care of this…"

Brooke growled and yanked back the blanket. Her hands took over as her teeth found Sam's lip and suddenly, Sam was wide awake.

A couple of hours later, despite the lack of sleep, Sam had a spring in her step when she left for work. She hadn't slept again after the most perfect way to wake up. She took the time after Brooke left to have a long shower, get ready, and read a little of her newest book. She was earlier than usual to work, but she wanted to finish early today to be on time for Finley's preschool event.

She was halfway through her morning when her phone rang. Lexi's number flashed on the screen, and she answered quickly, happy to hear from her. They talked on the phone every couple of days and texted sporadically. Sam loved getting to know more about her sister, surprising even herself with how easily she opened up to Lexi about her own life. She had never been so connected to someone so quickly, and she didn't know if it was the sisterly bond or just because she and Lexi got on really well, but she wasn't going to ruin it by overthinking.

"Hey, Sam. How are you?" Lexi's voice was a little shaky, and Sam frowned at the phone.

"I'm good. What's up? Is everything okay?"

The sigh on the other end made it apparent that no, it wasn't.

"Could we maybe meet up this evening? I need to talk to you."

Sam's heart beat faster, and she hated not knowing the cause. What could possibly have Lexi so rattled?

"I have a thing with Brooke and Finley tonight. What about tomorrow?"

Lexi took a moment to reply. "What about a late lunch today?"

Sam's alarm grew. Lexi was clearly in a rush to talk to her. "Is everything okay?"

Lexi took a deep breath and then blurted out, "It's about Valerie. Our mother. Same place for lunch? Please?"

Sam's heart stopped. She knew her mother's name, but in all their conversations, they hadn't called her by it. It was weird to hear out loud, outside the confines of her mind. What did Lexi know? What did she want to tell her? Did Sam even want to know? Funny how someone who you didn't even know could force your heart into a panic. Valerie...the word reverberated around her brain.

After Sam agreed to meet at two p.m., she signed off from Lexi, who clearly didn't want to say any more over the phone. Sam's head swam with the possibilities. Was she dead, had Lexi's dad found out? Was she alive and happy somewhere with another family? Did Sam have more siblings? Would she feel connected to them like she did Lexi? Her brain was on overload, all the possible scenarios circled around and around.

She considered ringing Brooke, but what would she say? Lexi might have some information about the woman who abandoned her and never looked back, but she didn't know what? Brooke would want her to ring, regardless of the lack of information, but she couldn't. She would either cry or spend time hypothesizing about what it might be, and neither option was going to help. So, she spent the next hour trying to lose herself in work and ended up at the café to meet Lexi fifteen minutes early.

Luckily, Lexi seemed just as eager, as five minutes later she slid into the booth across from Sam. They ordered lunch and caught up on each other's mornings until the waitress moved away. Sam was practically shaking by the time Lexi finally got to the reason they were there.

"I found her."

Sam took a moment before responding, "You found her? You were looking?"

Lexi nodded. "Around the same time, I started looking for you, I tried to find her. I had all but given up until yesterday. I left my number with a few of her old friends that Dad knew back in the day, in case she got in touch. I got a call from one of them last night to say they knew where she was. I got the information, but I haven't done anything about it yet. I wanted to talk to you."

Sam kept her breaths even. Lexi had information on where their mother was. They could probably go see her if they wanted to. Realistically, if it was an old friend, she was likely only a long car journey away. Even if she had disappeared to the other side of the country, that wasn't so hard to get to these days with the motorway. Sam would finally meet her, ask all the questions that haunted her into the early hours of the morning throughout her childhood.

"Where is she?" Sam's voice was barely above a whisper, but Lexi understood her.

"She's here, Sam. I don't think she ever left. She's living in a house about an hour outside the city."

Sam thought for a second that she misunderstood. But no, Lexi had been very clear. Valerie, their mother, was here, in the same place where Sam lived all her life. In the same place where she abandoned not one, but two daughters. She hadn't run far away from her mistakes, she had just…what? Forgotten about them?

"What do you want to do?"

Lexi shrugged. "I don't know. Part of me wants to see her, ask her why she left. Another part of me wonders if any answers she can provide will matter. It's never going to change it."

Sam agreed, and her brain was split with both of those thoughts too. She couldn't shake the feeling that she'd never be able to move on without at least seeing her...but what if it just made everything worse?

They spent the rest of the lunch talking around in circles about it, neither sure by the end of it what they wanted. They agreed to take some time to think about it before they made any decisions and would meet again at the weekend. Sam left the lunch with more questions than answers and spent the rest of the day lost in her head, the thoughts going from intrigued to downright terrified.

What if she met her mum and it confirmed everything that Sam had ever feared? That maybe, it really was her fault. That maybe, just maybe, Sam wasn't good enough.

❖

After work, Brooke picked Finley up from crèche, getting home in time to make something to eat before they had to leave for the school. Sam was going to meet them at the house in a few minutes, and they'd drive together. Her car pulled into the driveway right on time. As Sam walked through the door, Finley ran to her. She scooped him into her arms and tickled him as he squealed and giggled. He wrapped his arms around her neck, and Sam's eyes closed as she held him tight. Brooke swore tears glistened when Sam's eyes opened again.

Brooke looked at her questioningly, but Sam focused on Finley. She asked him questions about his day and made a big deal about how excited she was to see his school. Something was off, Brooke was sure of it, but she didn't have time to get into it right now. They needed to leave. In the car on the ride over, she tried to probe Sam to find out. Always the master of deflection, Sam didn't give a hint of what made those beautiful eyes look filled with sadness.

They walked into the preschool with Finley in the middle as he held both their hands. He clung close to them, looking interested but wary. There were quite a few kids and parents there already, and she could understand how overwhelmed he must be. They were greeted by someone who introduced herself as Maya; she would be Finley's teacher. She was friendly and enthusiastic. After a few of the right questions, Finley talked her ear off, taking her by the hand to a table filled with crayons and colouring sheets.

Brooke smiled; he would be just fine. She looked at Sam who also looked Finley's way. Her smile mirrored Brooke's but with that hint of sadness. She went to walk after Finley, but Brooke held her back. "Let's leave him to settle a bit and look around the room."

Sam looked hesitant. "Shouldn't we stay with him? He might get scared. What if he needs us?"

Brooke was about to make a joke, but there was genuine worry on Sam's face. "Sam, he'll be fine. We're in the same room, and he can find us anytime. Look at him. He's making friends already."

They watched for a moment as Finley joined a little girl at the table, who passed him a piece of paper and some crayons, and they both started to draw. Sam nodded, and they wandered around, looking at the posters on the wall.

Brooke had been unsure about where to choose for pre-school. This one was a little farther away than she would've liked, but they had sold her on the inclusion and diversity aspect. The brochures showed families of all types. Even the registration form requested pronouns and had two spaces for parent/guardian instead of mother and father like some of the others.

Finley was always comfortable to be whoever he wanted to be at home. That included playing with any toys he chose and wearing any clothes he wanted. Sometimes that meant dressing up as a cowboy and sometimes it meant dressing as a princess. He loved to play with dinosaurs and cars and also loved painting nails and taking care of his doll. Brooke made sure that he was never under pressure to be a certain type of person, and she needed him to be in an environment that had the same values. She wasn't foolish, she understood she was fighting an uphill battle when it came to keeping him from the pressure of gender in society, but she'd be damned if she didn't give it her all.

Sam pointed to a wall with the *My Family* colouring pages, and Brooke marvelled at the differences shown. It made her heart happy to see. They wandered back around to Finley, who was intently focused on his artwork.

"Whatcha doing there, buddy?" Sam bent down next to him as he glanced up and then back at the paper.

"Maya says we can all draw our families, and they go on that wall there."

Brooke smiled as he continued, and they spoke a little more with the teacher about what to expect when he started. She spoke to some of the other parents too until Finley was done.

"Ta-da!" Finley handed over his drawing with pride, a wide smile on his face. Brooke held it up as Sam peeked over her shoulder. She smiled brightly as she looked at what he had drawn.

Maya appeared to look and enquired, "Who is everyone, Finley?"

Finley's smile got wider as he pointed. "That's my mama, that's me, that's my Sammy, and that star is Daddy. He's the brightest star in the sky. My family."

Maya oohed and aahed over the masterpiece and hung it on the wall. Brooke turned to smile at Sam and noticed the tears slowly gathering in her eyes. Sam quickly swiped at them and picked up Finley as they got ready to go, holding him tight.

As Sam's whispered words reached Brooke's ears, her heart melted. "I love you, buddy."

CHAPTER TWENTY-TWO

Sam woke and reached out automatically for Brooke. Her eyes opened, and her heart sank as it hit her that she was alone, in her own bed. She had gotten used to waking up beside Brooke the past few days. It was her own fault.

Brooke invited her in after they got back from the pre-school, but Sam quickly made an excuse and headed home. When Brooke texted to ask what was wrong, Sam told her there was a problem with work and she was stressed. Why hadn't she told Brooke the truth?

But she knew why. Talking about it with Brooke would make everything seem more real. All the fears and thoughts that were trapped in her head would tumble out, and she was afraid she'd never shut the lid on it. She needed time to think about what she wanted, and she needed to do that alone.

After work that day, she rang Lexi. There was no point putting it off and letting it swim around her head until the weekend. There was only ever going to be one option. One way or another, she needed answers.

When Lexi picked up, she launched right into it before she could overthink. "Hey. Listen, I need to know more. I want to try to meet her. I'm happy to do it alone if you don't want to."

She took a breath and waited in anticipation. Although Sam would do it alone, having Lexi there would make it a whole lot easier.

"No, I want to. I need answers. Maybe we won't get any, but I need to at least try. Plus, I want to be there for my big sister."

Sam's heart clenched on hearing that, and she smiled. She was a big sister. In such a short time, Lexi had already become so important to her. "Good to hear, little sis."

She grinned despite the thumping of her heart at the idea of actually seeing their mother.

"So, what do we do?"

They talked for close to an hour and planned. They didn't have a phone number, just an address, so they would drive out on Saturday and simply knock, see who answered. Lexi had photos of their mum, so she knew what she looked like at least. Sam realized startlingly that she had no idea. She created so many pictures in her head throughout the years. So many stories of the life Valerie was living, the person she had become, how much she missed Sam and regretted leaving. Through every bad foster home, every scary night, she conjured up the woman who would one day tell her it was the biggest mistake of her life and love her once more.

Once they had a plan in place, they Google-Mapped the area and made sure they could park near enough to the house to wait if she wasn't home. They talked a bit about their fears. Lexi's father was apprehensive about the whole thing, but he supported what Lexi wanted. When they hung up with promises to check in the next day, Sam sat with her phone in her hand and pulled up Brooke's number.

Brooke would want to know. It was a big deal; she would be annoyed that Sam had kept it from her since yesterday. She would want to support Sam, would comfort her and take care of her. Brooke would be worried. There was no reason not to tell her, not to ring and share this news with her...what? Girlfriend?

She dialled the number and waited for Brooke to answer. Her hesitance was silly. Brooke was her best friend; she would want to be there for her right now. The call went to voicemail and Sam hung up. She checked the time. It was just after seven p.m., so Brooke was likely putting Finley to bed. She would wait until Brooke rang back and talk to her about it then.

After Sam made herself dinner, she sat in front of the television to eat and watch reruns of whatever happened to be on. She barely paid attention; her mind wandered onto what might happen this weekend. Would her daydreams come true? Would Valerie, the woman she had never gotten a chance to know, take her in her arms and cry? Sam allowed herself to imagine a tearful reunion. She would be angry, sure. Lexi would be, too. They would ask for answers that Valerie would give. Sam daydreamed that Valerie wasn't ready then to be their mother, but she was now. She'd gotten her life together. She wanted to be there for them.

Sam pulled up the house on Google Maps and looked at it again. It was a nice home. Modest. It could house a small family. Did Valerie have a new family? How would she feel about that? Sam would tell her about the foster homes. Valerie would feel bad; she would care. Ultimately, Sam would forgive her. She wanted to, needed to. They would create the bond that Sam always wanted.

It was close to ten when her phone rang. Sam was in bed with a book, an attempt to distract herself. Brooke's name flashed on the screen as she answered.

"Hey, I just saw your call."

At merely the sound of Brooke's voice, the ache in Sam's chest began to ease. "It's okay. Did you fall asleep with Fin again? How is the little gremlin?"

It was a running joke that on the rare occasion Finley took some time to get to sleep, Brooke fell asleep next to him. Many a night, Sam had to go wake her after waiting downstairs for Brooke to reappear.

"No, Dani came by when Fin went down so we were chatting, and I didn't even check my phone. Is everything okay?"

Sam frowned. "Dani called?"

Brooke paused, which was likely due to the tone Sam's voice had taken on. "Yeah. She texted me earlier to see if I wanted to have dinner. But with Fin, I just invited her over instead."

Sam had no rights to the jealousy lodged in her gut. She was aware that Brooke and Dani remained friends. It wasn't an issue. She trusted Brooke. It wasn't a big deal—and yet right now it was.

Sam couldn't help but feel like she needed Brooke earlier, yet Brooke was busy with Dani. Sam was fully aware of the irrational direction her thoughts took. Brooke hadn't known Sam needed her. She hadn't set out to make her feel bad. But Sam's mind was already on overload, and she couldn't stop herself as she spiralled into negativity.

"Okay. I'm going to bed now. I'll talk to you tomorrow."

All thoughts of telling Brooke everything disappeared. She needed to get her shit together before she said things that she didn't mean, and that Brooke certainly didn't deserve.

"Wait, Sam, is everything okay?"

Sam took a deep breath. Part of her knew she should just tell Brooke everything. Even the irrational thoughts in her head. Brooke would understand, she would reassure and comfort her. That's what she should do. Instead, Sam did what she always did. She hid. "Yeah, I'm just tired. Night, B."

Sam knew Brooke wanted to push further, but she wouldn't. Not while things were in this weird place between them. Her best friend Brooke would've called bullshit on her and demanded an explanation. But this new, hybrid version of their relationship made things different. Made them act differently.

"Okay. Well, text me when you wake, okay? Night, Sammy."

❖

By noon the next day, Brooke still hadn't received a reply from Sam other than one quick message to say she couldn't make lunch. Again. Brooke sighed in frustration. She was sure the weekend had solved a lot of their worries and weirdness. Now she knew something was wrong but had no idea what it possibly was. What had changed so drastically between Sunday and Monday evening?

Sam had been weird at the pre-school and then had practically run away afterward with a lame excuse about work. As if Brooke hadn't seen right through it. If Sam was freaked out about them again, she should at least clue Brooke in.

Brooke ruminated on how long she should leave it before she kicked Sam's ass. Or at least go by there and demand Sam talk to her. She considered ringing Maddie to ask her to collect Finley from crèche while she went over to Sam's after work, when her phone rang.

Brooke answered and made sure not to hide the annoyance in her tone. "Finally decided to tell me what the hell is going on?"

It came out angrier than intended but honestly, her patience was thin.

"Um, hello to you too."

Brooke waited, no reply necessary. Sam knew exactly why she was pissed; she didn't need to explain.

"I'm sorry. I know it was shitty to cancel on lunch. There's a lot going on and my head is a bit of a mess."

Brooke sighed. "Well, no shit. Maybe I'd understand a bit more if you actually bothered to talk to me about it."

Brooke moved from her desk and paced around her office, glad for the privacy she had.

"Well I tried, last night, but you were busy." Sam's voice was more sad than angry, but it held a hint of ice that made Brooke's blood run cold.

"Let's get one thing straight, Sam. Whatever this is between us, I am still my own person. I will be friends with whoever I want to be friends with, and I will not apologize for that. I never hid that I was spending time with Dani from you. I'm sorry you needed to talk, and I didn't see your call, but that gives you no right to take it out on me now."

She waited a beat until the soft sniffles came on the other end of the phone.

"I know, you're right. I'm lashing out. It's not about you, Brooke, I promise."

"Then what is it about, Sammy? Please, talk to me."

Sam's breaths on the other end were the only indication that the line hadn't cut off. The silence dragged on, but Brooke waited her out. She let her take all the time she needed.

Suddenly, Sam launched into the whole story. She started from Lexi calling her on Monday to the information about her mom and the decision to see her that weekend. She told Brooke about her worries and thoughts and fears, and Brooke listened. She asked a few questions along the way, but mostly, she just let Sam talk.

When Sam said all she needed to, Brooke wanted nothing more than to wrap her in her arms and protect her from the pain she was sure was to come. No matter the outcome of the weekend visit, it would hurt. "Come over tonight. Please. Let me take care of you."

Brooke waited, wondering if Sam would reject her offer. Sam was in the headspace where she sometimes thought she was better alone, not inflicting herself on others. It had happened many times throughout the years. Sometimes, days would go by where Sam shut herself off from the world, Brooke included. When it happened, pushing Sam only made her retreat even further. Usually, Brooke just waited her out. She couldn't, wouldn't do that this time. She needed to be there for her. This was too big.

"I'll be there at six. I'll bring food."

Brooke let out a breath and said goodbye. She sat back and contemplated all that Sam said. This was a huge step in Sam's life. When Lexi arrived in the picture, Brooke was worried too, but look how that turned out. Brooke had never known anyone to break through Sam's many barriers so quickly. Lexi was really good for her. Maybe her mother would be the same, although Brooke doubted it. This was the woman who walked out of Sam's life, leaving her with a father who clearly struggled with substance abuse and ultimately wasn't fit to take care of her. Neither of her parents deserved credit for the wonderful, smart, beautiful human that Sam had become.

Brooke was worried. Sam had been through so much already. Brooke had no idea how she even made it to who she was today. She hated seeing Sam hurt. Sam once admitted to her, a long time ago, that she had never known what it felt like to be truly wanted. That her biggest fear was that she never would. Her parents hadn't wanted her. Few of the foster families she had been placed with had wanted her beyond the money she brought them. Her first girlfriend had left without a second glance. Nobody had even tried to get close to her since then, until Brooke.

Brooke vowed to shower Sam with so much warmth, adoration, and comfort tonight that she never doubted how truly wanted she was.

CHAPTER TWENTY-THREE

It was early Saturday morning, the sun had yet to rise, but Brooke couldn't get her brain to shut off. Sam lay beside her in bed, gentle snores interrupting the otherwise silent morning. Sam had come over Wednesday as promised and stayed every night since. They talked about how Sam felt meeting her mum for what would be the first time that she remembered. They had spent every night talking, laughing, crying, and getting lost in each other before falling asleep together. Despite Sam's anxiety about meeting her mum, the time they spent together was perfect.

Brooke looked at Sam, her blond hair spread over the pillow and her face peaceful. Once Sam woke, the worry lines would appear on her forehead as she stressed about today. She ached to protect Sam from any pain she might feel but this was something Sam had to do.

Brooke offered to go with her, but Sam declined. Brooke wasn't offended; she knew Sam appreciated the offer but this was something Sam and Lexi needed to do together. Lexi called over Thursday night and the three of them talked, spent hours telling stories and laughing together. There was so much the sisters didn't know about each other, and Brooke was all too happy to fill Lexi in on some of Sam's antics.

Brooke had been careful to keep the affection strictly in the friend area when Lexi arrived. However, Sam soon made it clear that that was unnecessary. After Finley was in bed, she sat beside Brooke and held her hand. When Lexi raised an eyebrow, Sam was quick to inform her of their updated, yet unnamed, status. Her exact words had been, "We're still figuring it out."

But that was a good sign, right? That she wanted to share it with Lexi? It meant she wasn't hiding. They still kept it PG with Finley around for obvious reasons. They both sat him down for a chat about what he said to Maddie. He was still too young to really grasp anything other than Sam and his mama would sometimes go on dates now, and according to him, they went places together all the time anyway. If the time came for anything more official, they could talk to him, but for now, he was happy.

Sam began to stir, and Brooke stroked her hair gently. As her eyes flickered open, they locked on Brooke's and a small, sleepy smile appeared.

"Hey, sleepyhead."

Sam glanced at the clock and huffed. "Sleepyhead? It's six a.m. on a Saturday. Why are we awake?" Brooke chuckled and leaned over to kiss Sam's forehead, but Sam grabbed her and pulled her on top as she crushed their mouths together. "Actually, who cares why? Let's make the most of it before the toddler invasion occurs."

Brooke was unsure if Sam had yet to remember what was happening today or if she was trying to distract herself. Either way, it was best to go with it right now.

She kissed Sam deeply as Sam's hands began to wander. Her own followed suit, and it wasn't long before her body shuddered as Sam met her own release.

They both blissfully dozed when whirlwind Finley barrelled through the door, onto the bed, and wedged himself between them. "Pancakes?"

Brooke huffed a laugh. "You're going to turn into a pancake at this rate, little monster."

Finley giggled as Sam grinned across at her. "I can make them."

Brooke raised her eyebrows. "I think we established last time that you really cannot. I got this."

Not long after, they sat around the table, pancakes piled high and freshly cut fruit spread out. Sam laughed and joked with Finley and seemed like she hadn't a care in the world. She would fool almost anyone, except Brooke. The slight crease in her brow and the glazed look that overcame her when she began to think too much were an easy tell if you knew Sam like Brooke did.

Brooke waited until Finley ran off to play with his toys to broach the subject. Her hand slid easily into Sam's and she squeezed. "Nervous?"

Sam gulped, then nodded. "I just don't know what to expect." She squeezed Brooke's hand back tightly and rubbed her thumb along her palm. "What if she's happy and doesn't want reminders of her past mistakes? What if she's still who she was when she left? Do I want to bring that into my life? She'll still be my mother."

Brooke didn't have the words to make any of it better. There was no point in pretending that anything Sam worried about couldn't happen. All her fears and worries were valid and possible, Brooke knew this. She also knew that no matter what, Sam needed to find out.

"Listen. If she turns out to be someone you don't want to know, then you do not have any obligation to have that in your life. It will hurt, sure. But you owe her nothing. None of this 'she's your mother' crap." Brooke lifted Sam's chin to look into her eyes as she spoke. "Toxic people are toxic people, blood or not. And you've had enough toxic to last a lifetime. You have a family, Sam. You have me and Finley; we are your family and always will be, no matter what. Now you have Lexi too. You have your people, and you don't need her. But it could also end up being something that you want. She might end up being someone that you want to know."

Sam took a deep breath. "I'm just scared."

Brooke's heart cracked with the tears that entered Sam's eyes. She would give anything to change what happened to her, but she wouldn't change Sam for the world.

"I know. But at the end of the day, no matter what happens, you'll come back here, and I'll take care of you. Deal?"

Sam nodded again and looked into Brooke's eyes. "Thank you, B. For this past week, for everything. I don't know how I would've managed without you."

Brooke leaned in and brushed her lips against Sam's gently. "You would've managed just fine. You're the strongest person I know, Sammy. But luckily, you don't have to find out."

❖

As Sam got into Lexi's car to make the journey to their mother's house, her hands shook. Each mile that brought them closer made her heart beat a little bit faster. Lexi was unusually quiet, lost in her thoughts too. Sam wiped her sweaty palms off on her jeans and put them under her thighs to stop their movements.

She wondered what Valerie would look like. According to Lexi, or more accurately, Lexi's father, their mother had the same hair and eye colour as them which was no surprise.

Sam and Lexi looked so similar that she had to assume they took after Valerie. Sam asked to see the photo that Lexi had, in preparation, but it was long lost in piles of stuff in their garage. If Sam had a photo of their mother, would she have kept it somewhere to look at and imagine the life they might have lived? Lexi said it was easier to pretend it didn't exist. Just like their mother had done with them.

They arrived outside the house at ten a.m. Still early enough that she might be home, but not too early that she would likely be sleeping. They both looked at each other and took deep breaths.

"Whatever happens, we'll be okay, right?" Lexi sounded like she was trying to convince herself more than Sam, but Sam nodded anyway.

"We've made it this far. We'll be okay. We will try to get the information we came for and after that...well, at least we've found each other."

At that, Lexi pulled Sam into a hug. "I'm so glad I found you, Sam."

Sam held her sister tight and then pulled back. "Me too, but don't go getting me teary already."

Her misty eyes were proof that it was too late for that, but she laughed it off as they got out of the car and crossed the street.

The house looked almost exactly as it had on the maps. The garden was a little overgrown but not badly so. There was a car in the driveway which indicated that someone was home. Sam wasn't sure if that made her feel better or worse. That's what she came here for, right?

Sam braced herself and walked up to the red front door, rapping her knuckles against it before she had the chance to back out. It was now or never.

They waited for what felt like an age before footsteps sounded on the other side of the door. It opened, and suddenly, Sam was face to face with an older version of herself. That was the only way to describe it. She blinked, startled. When she first met Lexi, she couldn't get over seeing someone who looked so similar to her. But this woman was a carbon copy of Sam given twenty years.

Lexi grabbed her hand and squeezed as they all stared, saying nothing. The woman frowned, as if trying to figure out where she might know them from. Sam could see the exact moment it registered. Valerie's eyes widened and her mouth dropped open.

"How...what..." She stammered and trailed off. Sam felt sorry for her. At least they had time to prepare for this reunion, Valerie was blindsided.

"Can we come in?"

Valerie nodded and moved back. "Of course, of course. Come in. I'm sorry, I think I'm a little in shock."

You're not the only one, Sam thought. She walked into the house as Lexi trailed behind her. They were led into what was a modest but tidy living room. There was a small television set up in the corner, a couch, and an armchair. Sam sat on the couch, and Lexi sat beside her.

"Tea? Coffee?"

They both agreed to tea, and Valerie shuffled out to make it. It was the most surreal experience of her life. None of them had even acknowledged what was going on, but she was about to get served tea from the woman who abandoned her and set her life on the path she travelled alone for so very long.

Lexi gulped audibly beside her, still yet to utter a word. Sam jumped into big sister mode very easily, feeling a need to protect Lexi and take charge.

Lexi leaned into whisper, "She looks so much like us. Especially you. It's so weird."

Understatement of the year. It was true she looked more like Sam than Lexi in her other features. They had the same shaped face, similar build and height, whereas Lexi was taller and slimmer. Lost in her thoughts, she almost jumped when Valerie came back into the room, two cups in hand that she set on the coffee table in front of them.

She took the armchair across from where they sat and took a deep breath, as her hands shook in her lap. "I don't even know what to say."

At least she was being honest, Sam thought. So far.

"I'm guessing you know who we are?" Sam wanted to clarify the obvious, just in case.

"Of course I do. You're my girls. Samantha, look at you. And you, Alexis. You're so alike you could practically be twins."

Sam's throat clogged, and she took a few deep breaths.

"We go by Sam and Lexi." She pointed to herself when saying her name and then Lexi, just in case her mother didn't know which was which. It was likely. She hadn't looked directly at either of them when she spoke but more between the two

Valerie nodded. "I'm guessing you have questions you'd like to ask. I'll try my best to answer, but I can't promise I have the answers you're hoping to hear."

Sam was aware that would likely be the case. What answers would even matter right now? What would make any of this better?

Unless their mother was forced against her will to give them up and had fought to see them for their lives...nothing would be good enough. But she still had to know.

"Why did you leave?"

It was Lexi that asked the question that they all knew was coming. Sam grasped her hand as she heard the crack in her voice. Valerie took a moment before she answered.

"I wasn't capable of being a mother to you girls. When I left you, Samantha, Sam, I knew I could never be the person you needed. From the moment you were born, I knew you deserved better than me. I had a problem with drink, for longer than I care to remember. The best way I could take care of you was to leave. I figured your father would give you to his mother to raise. She always doted over you, and she could give you what I couldn't. She would love you like I hadn't been able to."

That last sentence sent a pain to Sam's gut. She was right all along. The simple fact was, she had been unlovable.

CHAPTER TWENTY-FOUR

The air had left Sam's lungs as her mother looked at her, not aware she had just said the words Sam feared hearing the most. Valerie continued before Sam had a chance to say anything, not that she had words to describe the ache in her chest.

"And you, Alexis—when I met your father, I knew he was a better person than I deserved. I let myself believe that, maybe this time, I was worthy of the love he gave me. When I got pregnant, I let myself get excited. Your father was over the moon despite the fact that neither of us were in a place to care for a child. But I tricked myself into thinking that maybe this time, I would do better. You arrived, and you were so beautiful, so precious. So much better than I deserved. I couldn't do it. I knew as the months went by and I felt no different than I had before that I wasn't made to be a mother."

Valerie paused, took a breath, and continued, clearly determined to get it all out in one go.

"Your father took to it easily, getting his act together bit by bit as I seemed to sink further into it. I stayed off alcohol, mostly, for both pregnancies but went straight back as soon as I could. I knew the best thing to do was leave. Your father would take care of you, I was sure of it, and he would find the happiness he deserved with someone else."

Although her hands still shook, Valerie's face looked almost void of emotion. It was like she had rehearsed this speech in the mirror, waiting for the occasion where she'd need to tell her story. Sam sat there, unable to even open her mouth.

"He did." Lexi's voice was raw but steady. "My father, he did take care of me. He did find happiness. He gave me everything you couldn't."

Valerie nodded, then looked at Sam expectantly.

"This was a mistake." Sam got up to flee toward the door.

Lexi followed her and grabbed her hand. "Sam, wait."

Sam's eyes were filled with tears, the hole that had been inside her for far too long gaped even wider than before.

"I can't, Lexi. This was a bad idea. I can't even look at her, sitting there waiting for absolution."

Valerie had yet to leave the armchair as Sam and Lexi stood in the doorway when she spoke again. "I don't expect anything from you, least of all forgiveness. I did the right thing with the capabilities I had at the time. I'm sure your grandmother has told you what an awful person I was back then. I couldn't have raised you, Sam."

Sam spun around and glared. "No, she didn't tell me. She didn't tell me anything. You left, and according to my social work files, which is the only information I have, my father tried to raise me by himself. He failed as miserably as I'm sure you'd expect. I was taken by social services when he left me alone in a car to get drugs in the middle of the night. Nobody came forward for me, nobody wanted me. I have no idea who my grandmother is or how much you believe she doted on me, but clearly, it wasn't enough to actually want me. I had nobody."

At that, Sam turned and walked out the door. She didn't bother to close it after her. She walked to the car, got in, and waited for Lexi who followed her out only minutes later. Her tears dried on her cheeks, replaced by an anger she couldn't shake. Her leg shook uncontrollably, and her throat clogged with so much emotion she couldn't begin to piece it apart. The world was suddenly far too loud, the car far too big, and her head far too full.

Lexi sat in silence with her, just being there. She didn't offer words meant to comfort or calm, she just sat. For that, Sam was grateful. After several deep breaths, she spoke. "You can go back in if you want. Ask whatever else you need. I can wait in the café down the road. You shouldn't miss out on getting the answers you came for just because of me."

At this, Lexi turned to face her. "She can't give us any answers. I doubt she even remembers the truth of what happened other than she left, and she's been trying to justify it to herself ever since. One thing I am grateful for is that she gave us each other. So, we can sit here for however long you need, or we can go get ice cream and forget about the world for a little while."

Sam's eyes swam with tears once more, but this time, there was more than the anger. Her head was full of pain and hurt and she felt like her worst nightmare had come true. That she was unwanted, unlovable, so much so that the one person in the world who should have loved her more than anything couldn't. But these tears held gratitude for the woman beside her who came into her life only a few weeks ago out of choice, out of a want to know who she was. Their mother might have given them the same blood, but they chose to be sisters. That meant everything.

She smiled a soft smile and managed to get out three simple words before the tears began to fall. "Ice cream, please."

❖

Brooke paced back and forth in the hallway. It had been hours since Sam left. She had gotten one text message just to say that she was okay and would talk to her later and nothing since. She sent Finley to his grandparents to stay overnight. She wanted to give her full attention to Sam, whatever the outcome.

The door opened and she stopped pacing as Sam walked through. Brooke immediately noticed her red-rimmed eyes and blotchy cheeks. Sam had been crying for a while, it seemed. Brooke moved toward her before she was even through the door fully and pulled her into her arms. As Brooke held her tightly, Sam started to cry again, soft tears that landed on Brooke's neck and soaked through her shirt. Brooke led her into the living room and onto the couch and pulled Sam into her lap as she held her close.

Sam hadn't uttered a word, and Brooke didn't ask anything. She just held her until the tears subsided, and Sam hiccupped that she had a headache. Likely from crying. Brooke led her upstairs and into bed. She got painkillers and water, made a hot water bottle, and shut the curtains, bringing the room into darkness. She pulled back the covers and crawled in beside Sam, rubbing her hair gently. A large part of her wanted so badly to know how it went. Were these tears of sadness for the years she lost with a person who might become something to her? Or were they tears of anger or hurt at the answers she had or hadn't gotten?

Brooke didn't ask. Sam would tell her when she was ready and now wasn't the time to push. They lay there in the dark until Sam's gentle snores reached Brooke's ears. She waited a little longer and then kissed her lightly on the forehead and went to get up, thinking she'd cook them dinner for when Sam was ready.

As she moved to leave the bed however, Sam gently whispered, "I was right."

Brooke turned and got back into the bed. "I thought you were sleeping. What do you mean, Sammy?"

Sam looked like she wanted to cry again but there were no tears left to fall. "I was right. She didn't want me. She didn't love me."

Her eyes looked devoid of emotion, as if she spoke about someone else's life. Brooke's heart sank into her chest as she reached out and put her arm around Sam.

"I'm so sorry. Do you want to talk about what she said?"

Sam raised her eyes and they looked cold, walls that Brooke hated seeing were right back in place. "That is what she said. Don't you understand? She didn't want me. Nobody wanted me. I had a grandmother, who apparently doted on me. My mother assumed she'd take me in. Because that's what family does, right? They take care of each other. But no, clearly, she didn't want me either. None of them did."

Brooke had no idea what to say. How did she respond to that? What words could she possibly offer to make this any easier for Sam?

"They missed out, all of them. On one of the best people that I've ever known. On the amazing light that you bring to everyone's lives. You are extraordinary, Sam. And that's despite them."

Sam's eyes closed and then opened again. Brooke sighed in relief. The vulnerability reflected at her was both a welcome sight and a heartbreaking one. Anything was better than the walls.

"I just want to feel wanted."

Sam's soft whispers were all Brooke needed. She moved toward her and rubbed her cheek with the palm of her hand gently. Her lips stopped inches from Sam's as she looked into her eyes. "I want you. Don't you see how much? Look at my eyes. Look at how you make me feel. I want you, Sam."

One lonely tear escaped and made its way down Sam's face as she closed the gap and pressed her lips to Brooke's.

They kissed softly at first and then with a passion that Brooke swore could set them on fire. Her body ached for Sam and her mind battled with the fact that Sam was vulnerable right now. As Sam pulled her on top and arched up against her, Brooke hesitated.

"Are you sure you want this right now?"

Sam didn't falter, she pulled Brooke closer and kissed her like her life depended on it.

"I'm sure. I need you, B. Please."

That was her undoing. Brooke made quick work of removing their clothes and spent what felt like hours kissing every inch of Sam's body. When Sam tried to touch her, Brooke stopped her.

"I want you. But right now, I want to show you how much. I want to take my time giving your body the attention it deserves, so relax and let me take care of you."

Sam gulped but relaxed back into the bed as Brooke did just that, working her hands, lips, tongue along every inch of glorious skin exposed to her. Sam was exquisite. Brooke knew that before, but right now, with the trust she bestowed upon Brooke, she was more beautiful than ever.

Brooke brought Sam to the height of bliss over and over, ignoring the ache between her own legs as she did her best to show Sam exactly how wanted she was. Finally, when Brooke couldn't wait any longer, she pressed her heated core against Sam's, brought their lips together, and slowly moved against Sam to bring them both to the peak once more. As she collapsed beside Sam and caught her breath, Sam turned and kissed her softly and slowly. Brooke gazed into the eyes that held so many emotions and so much depth and one thing was clear.

"I want you, Sam. You are so wanted, more than you'll ever know. I love you."

She'd said those three words to Sam many times over the years, but by the look on Sam's face, she knew that this time, they were different. Brooke held her breath as Sam stared at her, terrified of what Sam might say, or that she might say nothing at all. She didn't have long to wait until Sam opened her mouth and put her fears at ease.

"I love you, too."

CHAPTER TWENTY-FIVE

I'm not sure this is such a good idea."

Sam paced nervously as Brooke finished getting dressed.

"Sam, you've been to their house a million times. It would be weirder if you didn't come."

Sam stopped and looked at Brooke. "I've been to their house as your friend. Not as the woman who's now dating their son's widow."

Brooke rolled her eyes and gripped Sam's shoulders. "Will you stop for a minute? They love you. You know this. Maddie hasn't said anything to them yet, so if you're really uncomfortable, we can just keep it low-key. I won't lie to them, but I don't have to tell them anything outright."

Sam nodded and took a breath. "Yes, low-key, let's do that." Finley took that moment to run in wearing his adorable jeans, shirt, and bow tie. "Look at that style, kid. You're looking dapper."

Finley shrugged, and then his eyebrows raised. "Wow... Sammy, you look pretty."

Sam smiled and ruffled his hair, which was yet to be brushed. "Aww thanks, dude. Although you could sound a little less shocked."

He grinned and turned as Brooke walked out in her new black dress and heels. Sam gulped. "You look pretty too, Mama. Is this a three of us date?"

Brooke laughed. "I guess it sort of is."

Finley's smile split across his face. "I love three of us dates. Do you, Mama?"

Brooke nodded. "Of course I do, buddy."

"Even as much as you love going on dates with Sammy?"

Sam put her head in her hands as Brooke's cheeks reddened. "Low-key, huh?"

When they were finally ready to leave, Sam grabbed the present from the kitchen counter and headed to the car. It was Lila and Tom's anniversary, and they were holding a party at their house with close family and friends. Sam was nervous. She spent so much time with Lila and Tom over the years; they were like a surrogate family. They welcomed her with open arms when she began to spend more time with Brooke and Jacob. Once Finley came along and Jacob died, Sam spent almost as much time with them as Brooke did.

But how would they react to this new development between them? It wasn't going to be easy for them to see Brooke move on with anyone, let alone with someone who had been Jacob's friend.

They drove to the house and walked through the door, an excited Finley barrelled down the hallway to find his grandpa. They went into the kitchen to see the place already filled with people.

Maddie headed toward them and grinned. "I need to talk—"

Before she finished, Lila came up behind her. "Brooke, Sam, good to see you both."

She pulled them both into a hug and held on a little longer than usual. Sam frowned.

Maddie shrugged and disappeared into the crowd before Sam could ask her what she needed to talk about. Lila offered them food and drinks and went about fixing them plates from the buffet. She fussed over them like she always did. Something was different, though. Sam raised her eyebrows at Brooke, who shrugged. They mingled for a while, talking to aunts and uncles and cousins who they generally met once a year at Christmas and on the odd occasion.

Finley played video games with some of the older kids and was in his element. He didn't get to play them at home much, only the rare occasion Sam brought them over, so he loved getting to play at parties. Sam joined them for a while, kicking ass at *Mario Kart*. This was much more her style than the socialization side of things. Brooke found her a half hour later and dragged her away, with a good-natured eye roll.

"Lila has been looking for you."

Sam made her way into the kitchen to find her. Lila had heard about Lexi and wanted to talk to Sam about it. They got into a long conversation about not only that, but the meeting with her mother. Sam downplayed her feelings around it; it was a party, and she didn't want to put a damper on it. But Lila knew better than that and was way too easy to talk to. She managed to make her feel like everything would indeed be okay. Lila pulled her in for a hug, and Sam relaxed, her worries easing at the comfort.

"You've always got a family here, Sam. And anytime you need motherly advice, I'm here."

Sam's heart squeezed with a mixture of gratitude and guilt. Would Lila still say the same thing if she knew about her and Brooke? It wasn't long before she had her answer to that.

As Brooke joined them toward the end of the conversation, Tom appeared too and announced, "Well, if it isn't the new lovebirds."

Sam was sure she misheard. Brooke stuttered, "Wh-what?"

Lila smacked Tom lightly on the arm. "I was trying to be subtle, you dope."

Tom looked sheepish. "I was just trying to lighten the mood. You all looked far too serious."

Brooke shook her head. "Wait, you know?"

Lila rolled her eyes, and, in that moment, Sam could've sworn she really was Brooke's mother. "Of course we know. I know everything. Also, that grandson of mine has zero secret-keeping skills."

Sam's face was beetroot at this point and Brooke's wasn't far behind.

"We weren't keeping it a secret, as such. We were just waiting for the right time."

Lila smiled softly. "I know, dear. But there is never a wrong time for love."

It dawned on Sam that Lila knew all along, yet she hugged Sam and called her family regardless. She breathed deeply and smiled.

"So, you're okay with this?" There was still hesitation in Brooke's words, but Sam knew everything was going to be okay, just like Lila said earlier.

"Of course. There is nothing more we want than for you, for both of you, to be happy. That's exactly what Jacob would have wanted, too."

Sam's eyes were misty as she looked around her. Lila and Tom grinned at her, Brooke gazed at her lovingly, and Finley crept up and clung to Sam's leg. Maddie appeared and smiled, realizing what was going on. Here Sam was, surrounded by people who chose to love her. People who never had to want or accept her into their lives but did anyway. She suddenly felt like the luckiest person in the room. No matter how she had gotten here, she knew now that she was truly wanted.

❖

Later in the evening, Brooke and Sam ended up out on the swing set, taking a quick reprieve from the excitement. They swung back and forth in silence, staring up at the stars. Brooke broke the silence first.

"I can't believe they are so okay with it."

Sam turned to look at her. "Hey, you said they would be."

Brooke shrugged. "I was trying to make you feel better. I had no idea how they'd actually react. I definitely didn't expect this level of understanding."

Sam huffed and then laughed. "Yeah, they are pretty great. Jacob got lucky with them."

Brooke nodded. "He knew it, too. We used to joke about how our mothers were so opposite. Lila has always been so involved in everything; Jacob used to complain about it, but he knew he was lucky. My mother did her best, but she was always more interested in herself."

Brooke reached out for Sam's hand. "I'm sorry, I shouldn't complain. Considering…"

Sam shook her head and cut her off quickly. "No. You get to complain. My experiences don't negate yours. Just because my mother disappeared, it doesn't make your mother's disinterest any easier."

Brooke wrapped her arms around Sam and pulled her close. "Thank you, Sammy."

She marvelled at the ease of their new dynamic now. In a relatively short space of time, their whole relationship had shifted on its axis and yet, it was still the same in so many ways. When she met Jacob, she knew it was going to be something. She knew almost immediately that they were special, and she was right. They spent years of happiness together and created a beautiful, kind, funny child who was her world. When Jacob was taken, Brooke was sure that was it for her. She was done; she'd had her one true love and that was that.

When she met Sam all those years ago, she knew they were meant to be in each other's lives. She spent so long trying to convince Sam of that fact for reasons she couldn't explain, other than she knew they needed each other. Again, she was right. She didn't know what they would become, but she was so glad she didn't give up on Sam.

The love she had for Jacob would never be replaced, but what she had with Sam was just as strong. It was different, but no less special or intense. Love really didn't have a limit. Her heart was big enough to hold more than she ever anticipated, and right now it was bigger than ever before.

Sam looked at her then and smiled, kissing her softly. "Thinking too much again?"

Brooke smiled right back, shaking her head. "All good thoughts. I'm just thinking about how I'm the luckiest woman in the world right now."

Sam kissed her once more and then shrugged. "Sorry, you're wrong. It's rare but it happens. Because that title belongs to me."

Just then, Finley burst out the door and ran toward them. "There is gonna be cake soon!"

He was a bundle of sugar and excitement; he loved cake almost as much as pancakes. Brooke scooped him up and plopped him on her lap, Sam's arms still around her, now encompassed them both.

"Is that right, buddy? Well, we better get some cake then."

But she made no effort to move. Instead she sat, Sam's arms around them and her son in her lap, looking up into the sky filled with stars as the darkness encompassed them. She basked in the beauty of the night, of her life. Her heart was so full of so many things but more than anything, gratitude.

CHAPTER TWENTY-SIX

S am grabbed some clothes in a bag from her apartment,
the little that still remained there, before she headed
over to Brooke's. She had stayed there almost every night for the
past month, since before the meeting with her mother. Despite
everything that happened that weekend, life had been good. Brooke
was amazing. It was everything Sam ever dreamed of and more.
They spent most days just like they always had, but the nights…
the nights were everything.

Finley loved having Sam around more, and they still made a
point of going on their date days. Sam put him to bed most nights
with Brooke, and as they read stories and she kissed him good
night, she couldn't imagine ever not being there for him. She
couldn't imagine ever walking away. She realized over those few
weeks what a privilege it was to never have to.

Maddie was happy to babysit when they needed some alone
time. Date nights had mainly been spent in Sam's apartment; the
only times she stayed here was when Brooke stayed right beside
her. Life had been messy and complicated the past few months, but
she wouldn't change it for the world.

Even the stuff with Valerie. No, she hadn't gotten the reunion
of her dreams, but she got closure. She had gone back to her
therapist a week after the party and talked with Brooke too. She
opened up more over the evenings together, determined to face

her fears head on this time to give them the best shot possible. She finally processed that it was never about her. Valerie didn't have the ability to be a mother, but that wasn't Sam's fault. It wasn't anything to do with her at all.

As she grabbed her keys to walk out the door, her phone rang. "Hey, Lexi, what's up?" Lexi sniffled and Sam immediately stopped rushing. "Lexi, what's the matter?"

Lexi took a deep breath. "Can you meet me? Please?"

Sam didn't hesitate. "Of course. Want to meet me at Brooke's? I'll be there in fifteen minutes."

After Lexi agreed, Sam signed off and hopped in her car. What happened to make Lexi so upset? Her heart clenched at the idea of something hurting her sister. It was so strange that only a few short months ago, Sam hadn't even known she had a sister, and now the mere consideration of something upsetting Lexi made her fiercely protective.

She pulled into Brooke's driveway and got her bag from the car. She reached the front door just as Lexi pulled in behind her car. Sam waited, door open, for Lexi to make her way up to her. Red-rimmed eyes and tear-stained cheeks pulled at Sam's heart. Sam wrapped her arms around her sister and held her tight before she led Lexi into the living room. Brooke was still at the Fields' house with Finley; she was due back in about an hour.

Sam settled Lexi on the couch and made them tea, then sat beside her. "What's going on, Lexi?" Lexi sniffled again and looked up at Sam. "I went to see her again. I'm sorry. I just…I needed to know more." Sam's heart sank. Their mother. Valerie did this.

"Don't apologize, Lexi. She's your mother too. You have a right to have a relationship with her, even if I don't want one."

Lexi shook her head. "You were right. Nothing has changed. I went into the house, and she was rambling about how she did the right thing and you just didn't understand. She was going on about how hard it all was for her and how lucky we both were because we had each other. She even said we should thank her for it, as if she did us a favour. I went into the kitchen to get to the bathroom and there were bottles of vodka on the counter. She was drunk—of course she was. I knew all along. I was just trying to convince myself it wasn't true—that she had changed. But nothing has changed."

Sam pulled Lexi into a hug. "I'm sorry, Lexi. I really hoped I was wrong, for you. I wish it was different."

Lexi held her tight. "I should've known. I walked out and got in my car and rang you."

Sam sat back and smiled softly. "I'm glad you did. Honestly, I feel sorry for her. Valerie is alone, and she clearly has issues that for whatever reason, she hasn't been able to face outside of numbing them with alcohol. She left us, but she left herself too. I can't imagine how lonely that must be. But she made her choices and now, we get to make ours. And I choose to focus on the family that loves me and shows that they care about me time and time again. You included."

Lexi nodded as she dried her tears. "You're right. I know you are. I have my dad, his family, you, Brooke, and Fin. I have amazing friends. I don't need her."

They talked longer until Brooke came back with Finley. She sensed immediately that something was off and set to work preparing dinner, comfort food to cheer them all up. They spent the evening eating and chatting, and it turned out to be a wonderful time.

As Lexi went to leave, she hugged Sam tightly. "Thanks, Sam. I felt so bad on the way here and now I'm just thankful. For you, and for Brooke's cooking of course."

Sam laughed; she couldn't argue with that.

"Oh. Here, she gave me this for you. Before the rambling." Lexi handed over an envelope to Sam, her name printed across it in an unfamiliar script. It must be Valerie's handwriting, something she'd never seen before.

After Lexi left, Sam walked back into the kitchen holding it as Brooke walked toward her. They had filled Brooke in once Finley was in bed on what happened, so she knew why Lexi was upset.

Sam held up the envelope. "From Valerie," she mumbled as a way of explanation. They sat on the couch together as Sam stared at it.

"Are you going to open it? Do you want to be alone?"

Sam shook her head and held Brooke's hand. "I'll open it, but I want you here."

"I'm not going anywhere."

Sam opened the envelope and removed a sheet of notebook paper dated about a week ago. She scanned the letter quickly, then read both sides as a tear tracked down her cheek. When she finished, she folded it back up and put it on the side table.

Sam sat in silence for a moment, and Brooke waited patiently.

"She says that she went to see my grandmother, to get answers for me. A neighbour said that she died. Twenty-six years ago, which would be three months before I was taken by social services. The neighbour was an old family friend. According to her, my grandmother had cared for me. I spent most of my time with her after my mother left and only went back to my father when she passed away. She was planning to apply to have me full time, legally."

Tears streamed down Sam's face as she looked at Brooke. "She says other stuff about herself and her choices, most of the same as what she said to Lexi. But, Brooke—my grandmother— she wanted me. She fought for me. She loved me."

Sam wiped the tears from her eyes as Brooke pulled her close and held her tight. Part of her ached for the life she might have had if her grandmother had lived. But mostly, she clung to the part that resounded in her head that she was wanted. She was loved. She always had been, right from the start, someone fought for her.

"What are you going to do about your mother?"

Sam shrugged. "Nothing. You said it before, and you were right. I owe her nothing. I feel bad for her and the life she lives, but she has a roof over her head and she clearly has money to drink, so I don't feel obligated to do anything about it. I have a family, I have so many people who love me, and that's despite her. That's what I need to focus on."

Brooke held her close as Sam thought of the grandmother she couldn't remember, and a little crack in her heart began to heal.

❖

Brooke laughed, taking another bite of food while Dani finished telling the story of her latest art exhibition and the antics that went on between two of the purchasers about one particular piece. Sam sat at her other side and laughed along with her. Brooke was happy Sam didn't find it weird having Dani here for lunch.

As they finished lunch and Dani got up to leave, Finley came through the door followed by Maddie. They went for ice cream, and by the looks of it, stopped at the toy shop on the way home.

"Hey, kiddo." Dani high-fived Finley as he passed to jump into Sam's arms to show her his new Lego set. Brooke rolled her eyes as she turned toward Maddie. "I said no toys." Maddie had the grace to look sheepish and shrugged. "He talked me into it. I couldn't help it."

After Brooke returned from walking Dani out, Sam and Finley were already seated at the table, started on the Lego set. Maddie left shortly after, on the way to meet Carl.

Brooke joined them at the table and looked at Sam. "Now?" she mouthed. Sam widened her eyes and shrugged, going back to focus on the Lego set. Brooke huffed a sigh. "Fin, we need to talk to you for a second." Finley continued to search for the piece he needed and barely glanced up.

"Finley, look at me for a second." She nudged Sam, who stopped building sheepishly and sat up. Finley followed suit. Brooke took a breath and ploughed on. "Sam and I...we...well, we wanted to tell you something. You know how we have been going on dates and Sam has been staying here more? Well, how would you feel if Sam stayed here all of the time? If she lived with us?"

Finley looked confused, his brows furrowed as he glanced between the two of them. Brooke was irrationally nervous as she waited for him to reply.

"Sammy already lives with us, silly."

Brooke let out a breath and laughed. "Well, not exactly, buddy. She would move in here for real with all her stuff and be here every night." Finley shrugged, then his eyes lit up. "All her stuff? Like the big Legos that Sam has in her apartment? And the video games?"

Sam chuckled and nodded as Brooke rolled her eyes at her son's priorities. She was about to be outnumbered. They spent the rest of the evening with Sam and Finley building Legos as Brooke read a book, checking in on them from time to time. It was blissfully peaceful. Having Sam here not only meant they had more time together, it also gave Brooke time to herself while Finley was happy and entertained with someone who loved him.

They put Finley to bed together that night. After they read his story, he cuddled in and looked up at them from his twin bed.

"Mama? Sammy?"

They both looked at him expectantly. He looked so tiny in the bed. He acted so grown up sometimes that she forgot how little he really was.

"I love our family."

Brooke leaned down and kissed his forehead as he closed his eyes. "Me too, monkey." Sam wiped a stray tear from her eye. Brooke slid her hand into Sam's, and they walked out of the room.

"He's gotta be the best kid in the world. I know I'm biased but seriously, he's the best."

Brooke pushed Sam up against the wall and silenced her as she pressed their lips together hard. God, she never got enough of this. Sam matched her pace and gripped her hips, pulling her closer.

"I need you. Now."

Brooke pulled Sam into her bedroom—their bedroom, she mentally corrected herself. Sam took over and pushed Brooke back onto the bed, pulling off her pants before she buried her head between Brooke's legs. Too eager to wait.

Brooke gripped the back of Sam's head as her thighs wrapped around Sam's shoulders, and she moaned. Sam's tongue darted in and out and then circled around where Brooke ached for her. It didn't take long before Brooke's legs shook, and Sam crawled up her body to kiss her while she came down. She knew the night would end like many other nights over the past few months, with both of them sated and blissful, curled up together, exhausted, and happy.

She spent the next while bringing Sam the same pleasure she just received and loved every moment. They threw on a movie as Sam laid her head on Brooke's shoulder with her leg thrown over Brooke's. Brooke kissed Sam's head as she laughed at one of the lines in the movie, and she couldn't understand how she had gotten so lucky.

She glanced around her room, their room, and took in the changes. Sam's clothes strewn over the back of the chair. Her many gadgets on the nightstand beside her. Some frames waiting to be hung on the wall, having come from Sam's apartment. So many subtle changes, but none as big as the change inside Brooke.

There was no niggling voice. No guilt. No worry about the future, or regret about the past. There was just peace. Acceptance. Love. So much love. Brooke knew that life was messy, painful, all too often excruciating. But sometimes, it was better than she could ever have expected. With Sam in her arms, life suddenly seemed full to the brim with possibilities.

EPILOGUE

Two years later

"Mom. Mom! Come on. Mama is waiting."

Sam turned and grinned at her adorable five-year-old son. Finley looked handsome in his suit and red bow tie as he hopped from foot to foot with excitement.

"Whoa, you look like a princess."

Her heart warmed at his words, and she turned back to look in the mirror. She did look like a princess. Her ivory lace jumpsuit was threaded with red ribbon, matching Finley's bow tie. Lexi stood to the side of her in her red lace dress, a wide grin on her face.

"You ready?"

Sam nodded, grasping Lexi's hand to pull her in for a hug. She had never been more ready for anything in her life. They walked out the door and down the hall, hand in hand with Finley. Lexi led the way outside and onto the small, private beach. They'd spent months picking the perfect place, and the minute they stepped foot here, they knew this was it. It was perfect, small and intimate, just what they wanted.

As Sam walked down the cobbled pathway toward the group of people on the beach, her heart was so full. Lexi walked up the aisle first, and Sam followed with Finley on her arm. His chest was puffed out, and he looked happier than ever. They passed his grandmothers, both sets of eyes tearing up already. Dani was there too, a wide smile brightened her face as they passed. They reached the top of the aisle next to Lexi as Sam turned.

Her eyes locked on the figure that walked toward her, arm in arm with Tom who looked so proud. Maddie walked in front of Brooke in a dress that matched Lexi's. Sam couldn't take her eyes off Brooke. Her dress was similar to Sam's jumpsuit in material but a completely different design. It was exquisite. She was perfect.

As Brooke reached her, she took her hands and stared into her eyes. It took all Sam's willpower not to kiss her right then. The celebrant went through the ceremony, and Sam barely took in a word of it, too engrossed in the woman in front of her. Her skin tingled as she waited to hear the words she longed for.

"You may now kiss the bride."

She didn't need any further encouragement. She pulled Brooke close and pressed their lips together, only holding back because they were in the presence of family. Her family. She looked around at the people who were so happy for her and knew that she was, without a doubt, loved. She looked into Brooke's smouldering eyes and knew that she was, without a doubt, wanted. Finley ran to them and wrapped his arms one around each of them, and Sam held everything that she'd ever needed right there in her arms.

❖

Brooke laughed as she watched her wife and son on the dance floor. Her wife. She would never get sick of that. Dani came up beside her and hugged her tightly. "You look beautiful. And so, so happy."

Brooke grinned. "I am. I really am." They watched as Sam twirled Finley around in circles. "Good thing you blew it with me, eh?" Brooke laughed at the reminder of the start to all of this. "How is Ruby doing?" A small smile played on Dani's lips. "Good, she's back in town next week, and we're going to grab dinner. I haven't seen her in a long time."

Brooke took in the wistful look that appeared on Dani's face. There was more to Dani and Ruby than the friends they claimed to be, but time would tell. Maybe Brooke would get to return the favour soon and give Dani the wake-up call she'd given Brooke. Right now though, she had more important things to think about.

She walked onto the dance floor and scooped Finley into her arms as Sam wrapped her arms around them. They danced, laughed, and held each other tight as Brooke sang horribly off-key to the song. They all soon got tired and grabbed some drinks.

The sun began to set as Sam grabbed Brooke's hand and pulled her out of the gazebo they had set up for dinner and onto the beach. They walked hand in hand as the stars came out and twinkled in the sky. Brooke gazed at Sam's face, as beautiful in the moonlight as it was in the sun. She would never get used to this.

"You're my wife."

It was a simple statement that sent Brooke's heart into a flutter.

"And you're mine."

"Always."

They stood, simply smiling at each other when arms wrapped around them from behind. Finley had made his way over to them and hugged them tightly. They sat in the sand, wedding attire be damned, and Brooke pulled Finley into her lap. Sam held them both close.

"Look! It's Daddy."

They stared up at the brightest star in the sky. Brooke smiled. "Yeah, monkey, it is."

Sam held them both tighter as her smile widened. Brooke gazed at the star and then turned to face Sam as Finley curled up in her lap. She kissed Sam softly and thanked whatever force brought this amazing woman into her life. They sat together, the three of them full to the brim with happiness, beneath the twinkling stars.

The End

About the Author

J.J. Hale has been devouring books since she was able to hold one and has dreamt about publishing romance novels with queer leading ladies since she discovered such a thing existed, in her late teens.

The last few years have been filled with embracing and understanding her neurodiversity, which has expanded the dream to include representing kick-ass queer, neurodivergent women who find their happily ever afters.

Jess lives in the south of Ireland, and when she's not daydreaming, she works in technology, plays with LEGO, and (according to the kids) fixes things.

Website: www.jjhaleauthor.com
Email: jjhaleauthor@gmail.com
Twitter: @OverthinkerJess
Facebook & Instagram: @jjhaleauthor

Books Available from Bold Strokes Books

A Cutting Deceit by Cathy Dunnell. Undercover cop Athena takes a job at Valeria's hair salon to gather evidence to prove her husband's connections to organized crime. What starts as a tentative friendship quickly turns into a dangerous affair. (978-1-63679-208-8)

As Seen on TV! by CF Frizzell. Despite their objections, TV hosts Ronnie Sharp, a laid-back chef; and paranormal investigator Peyton Stanford, have to work together. The public is watching. But joining forces is risky, contemptuous, unnerving, provocative—and ridiculously perfect. (978-1-63679-272-9)

Blood Memory by Sandra Barret. Can vampire Jade Murphy protect her friend from a human stalker and keep her dates with the gorgeous Beth Jenssen without revealing her secrets? (978-1-63679-307-8)

Foolproof by Leigh Hays. For Martine Roberts and Elliot Tillman, friends with benefits isn't a foolproof way to hide from the truth at the heart of an affair. (978-1-63679-184-5)

Glass and Stone by Renee Roman. Jordan must accept that she can't control everything that happens in life, and that includes her wayward heart. (978-1-63679-162-3)

Hard Pressed by Aurora Rey. When rivals Mira Lavigne and Dylan Miller are tapped to co-chair Finger Lakes Cider Week, competition gives way to compromise. But will their sexual chemistry lead to love? (978-1-63679-210-1)

The Laws of Magic by M. Ullrich. Nothing is ever what it seems, especially not in the small town of Bender, Massachusetts, where a witch lives to save lives and avoid love. (978-1-63679-222-4)

The Lonely Hearts Rescue by Morgan Lee Miller, Nell Stark, Missouri Vaun. In this novella collection, a hurricane hits the Gulf Coast, and the animals at the Lonely Hearts Rescue Shelter need love, and so do the humans who adopt them. (978-1-63679-231-6)

The Mage and the Monster by Barbara Ann Wright. Two powerful mages, one committed to magic and one controlled by it, strive to free each other and be together while the countries they serve descend into war. (978-1-63679-190-6)

Truly Wanted by J.J. Hale. Sam must decide if she's willing to risk losing her found family to find her happily ever after. (978-1-63679-333-7)

A Good Chance by Ali Vali. Harry, Desi, and Desi's sister Rachel are so close to getting everything they've ever wanted, but Desi's ex-husband is coming back to get his revenge and rip apart their chance at happiness. (978-1-63679-023-7)

A Perfect Fifth by Jaycie Morrison. Streetwise pianist Zara Keller and Lady Jillian Stansfield couldn't be more different; yet their connection brings a new awareness of who they are and what they truly want in their lives—including each other. (978-1-63679-132-6)

Catching Feelings by Ana Hartnett Reichardt. Andrea Foster expected to catch a lot of pitches from the Alder Lion's star pitcher, Maya, but she didn't expect to catch feelings. (978-1-63679-227-9)

Defiant Hearts by Lee Lynch. In these stories, you'll find your lovers, friends, and lesbians you wish you knew—maybe even yourself. (978-1-63679-237-8)

Love and Duty by Catherine Young. All Princess Roseli wants is to marry her three lovers, but with war looming, she must instead marry Princess Lucia to establish a military alliance between their planets. (978-1-63679-256-9)

Murder at Union Station by David S. Pederson. Private Detective Mason Adler struggles to determine who killed a woman found in a trunk without getting himself killed in the process. (978-1-63679-269-9)

Serendipity by Kris Bryant. Serendipity brings jingle writer Annie Foster and celebrity pop star Bristol Baines together, and their undeniable attraction keeps them close, but will their different paths drive them apart? (978-1-63679-224-8)

The Haunted Heart by Jane Kolven. A ghost, a ring, and a quest to find a missing psychic—it's a spell for love. (978-1-63679-245-3)

The Rules of Forever by Nan Campbell. After reconnecting at their high school reunion, Cara and Lauren agree to embark on a textbook definition friends-with-benefits relationship, but trying to keep it uncomplicated is harder than it seems. (978-1-63679-248-4)

Vision of Virtue by Brey Willows. When virtue and desire come together, be prepared for sparks in this next installment of the Memory's Muses series. (978-1-63679-118-0)

Cherry on Top by Georgia Beers. A chance meeting leaves Cherry and Ellis longing for a different life, but when Ellis's search for truth crashes into Cherry's insta-filter world, do they have any hope at all of a happily ever after? (978-1-63679-158-6)

Love and Other Rare Birds by Angie Williams. Ornithologist Dr. Jamie Martin and park ranger Rowan Fleming are searching the Alaskan wilderness for a bird thought to be extinct and they're about to discover opposites really do attract. (978-1-63679-108-1)

Parallel Paradise by Mayapee Chowdhury. When their love affair is put to the test by the homophobia of their family, community, and culture, Bindi and Rimli will need to fight for a chance at love. (978-1-63679-204-0)

Perfectly Matched by Toni Logan. A beautiful Cupid named Hannah, a runaway arrow, and just seventy-two hours to fix a mishap that could be the best mistake she has ever made. (978-1-63679-120-3)

Royal Exposé by Jenny Frame. When they're grouped together for a class assignment, Poppy's enthusiasm for life and love may just save Casey's soul, but will she ever forgive Casey for using her to expose royal secrets? (978-1-63679-165-4)

Slow Burn by Missouri Vaun. A wounded wildland firefighter from California and a struggling artist find solace and love in a small southern town. (978-1-63679-098-5)

The Artist by Sheri Lewis Wohl. Detective Casey Wilson and reclusive artist Tula Crane are drawn together in a web of passion, intrigue, and art that might just hold the key to stopping a killer. (978-1-63679-150-0)

The Inconvenient Heiress by Jane Walsh. An unlikely heiress and a spinster evade the Marriage Mart only to discover true love together. (978-1-63679-173-9)

A Champion for Tinker Creek by D.C. Robeline. Lyle James has rescued his dad's auto repair business, but when city hall condemns his neighborhood, Lyle learns only trusting will save his life and help him find love. (978-1-63679-213-2)

Closed-Door Policy by Erin Zak. Going back to college is never easy, but Caroline Stevens is prepared to work hard and change her life for the better. What she's not prepared for is Dr. Atlanta Morris, her gorgeous new professor. (978-1-63679-181-4)

Homeworld by Gun Brooke. Headed by Captain Holly Crowe, the spaceship Velocity's crew journeys toward their alien ancestors' homeworld, and what they find is completely unexpected—and they're not safe. (978-1-63679-177-7)

Outland by Kristin Keppler & Allisa Bahney. Danielle Clark and Katelyn Turner can't seem to stay away from one another even as the war for the wastelands tests their loyalty to each other and to their people. (978-1-63679-154-8)

Secret Sanctuary by Nance Sparks. US Deputy Marshal Alex Trenton specializes in protecting those awaiting trial, but when danger threatens the woman she's falling for, Alex is in for the fight of her life. (978-1-63679-148-7)

Stranded Hearts by Kris Bryant, Amanda Radley, Emily Smith. In these novellas from award winning authors, fate intervenes on behalf of love when characters are unexpectedly stuck together. With too much time and an irresistible attraction, anything could happen. (978-1-63679-182-1)

The Last Lavender Sister by Melissa Brayden. Aster Lavender sells her gourmet doughnuts and keeps a low profile; she never plans on the town's temporary veterinarian swooping in and making her feel like anything but a wallflower. (978-1-63679-130-2)

The Probability of Love by Dena Blake. As Blair and Rachel keep ending up in the same place despite the odds, can a one-night stand turn into forever? Or will the bet Blair never intended to make ruin their happily ever after? (978-1-63679-188-3)

Worth a Fortune by Sam Ledel. After placing a want ad for a personal secretary, a New York heiress is surprised when the woman who got away is the one interested in the position. (978-1-63679-175-3)

A Fox in Shadow by Jane Fletcher. Cassie's mission is to add new territory to the Kavillian empire—murder, betrayal, war, and the clash of cultures ensue. (978-1-63679-142-5)

Embracing the Moon by Jeannie Levig. Just as Gwen and Taylor are exploring the new love they've found, the present and past collide, threatening the future they long to share. (978-1-63555-462-5)

Forever Comes in Threes by D. Jackson Leigh. Efficiency expert Perry Chandler's ordered life is upended when she inherits three busy terriers, and the woman she's referred to for help turns out to be her bitter podcast rival, the very sexy Dr. Ming Lee. (978-1-63679-169-2)

Heckin' Lewd: Trans and Nonbinary Erotica by Mx. Nillin Lore. If you want smutty, fearless, gender-diverse erotica written by affirming own-voices folks who get it, then this is the book you've been looking for! (978-1-63679-240-8)

Missed Conception by Joy Argento. Maggie Walsh wants a relationship with Cassidy, the daughter she's only just discovered she has due to an in vitro mix-up. Heat kindles between Maggie and Cassidy's mother in a way neither expects. (978-1-63679-146-3)

Private Equity by Elle Spencer. Cassidy Bennett spends an unexpected evening at a lesbian nightclub with her notoriously reserved and demanding boss, Julia. After seeing a different side of Julia, Cassidy can't seem to shake her desire to know more. (978-1-63679-180-7)

Racing the Dawn by Sandra Barret. After narrowly escaping a house fire, vampire Jade Murphy is unexpectedly intrigued by gorgeous firefighter Beth Jenssen, and her undead existence might just be perking up a bit. (978-1-63679-271-2)

Reclaiming Love by Amanda Radley. Sarah's tiny white lie means somehow convincing Pippa to pretend to be her girlfriend. Only the more time they spend faking it, the more real it feels. (978-1-63679-144-9)

Sol Cycle by Kimberly Cooper Griffin. An encounter in a park brings Ang and Krista together, but when Ang's attempts to help Krista go spectacularly wrong, their passion for each other might not be enough. (978-1-63679-137-1)

Trial and Error by Carsen Taite. Attorney Franco Rossi and Judge Nina Aguilar's reunion is fraught with courtroom conflict, undeniable chemistry, and danger. (978-1-63555-863-0)